A DREAMER'S ROMANCE

Other books by Judy Kouzel:

Her Lifelong Dream

A DREAMER'S ROMANCE

•

Judy Kouzel

AVALON BOOKS
NEW YORK

Published by Thomas Bouregy & Co., Inc.
160 Madison Avenue, New York, NY 10016

Library of Congress Cataloging-in-Publication Data

Kouzel, Judy.
    A dreamer's romance / Judy Kouzel.
        p. cm.
    ISBN 0-8034-9773-3 (acid-free paper)
    1. Booksellers and bookselling—Fiction. I. Title.

    PS3611.O7494D74 2006
    813'.6—dc22

                                        2005033807

PRINTED IN THE UNITED STATES OF AMERICA
ON ACID-FREE PAPER
BY HADDON CRAFTSMEN, BLOOMSBURG, PENNSYLVANIA

To Beverly Kouzel

Chapter One

The woman in the navy blue pea coat arrived at Brian's Books & Coffee Shop at eight o'clock sharp, just as she'd done every Friday night for the past three months. Brian watched her as she walked to the back of the store and into the mystery section, where she began to browse through the two spinning racks of paperback novels. He knew she'd spend the next hour carefully examining the books before she finally made her selection.

Brian pretended to study his clipboard while he stole glances at the pretty young woman. "What's a woman like that doing alone on a Friday night?" he wondered, as he'd wondered every Friday night since the first time he laid eyes on her. He shook his head and shrugged.

Brian McKenzie was a handsome man but was fully unaware of his good looks. He had thick chestnut brown hair, which he wore short, and intense gray-blue eyes that sometimes squinted when he was deep in

1

thought. He was taller than average, with broad shoulders and a fit, athletic build. He didn't diet or have a regular exercise program. Instead, he stayed in shape by riding his bicycle the twelve miles to and from the bookstore. He was also passionate about any activity that allowed him to be near the water—fishing, kayaking, and sailing were his favorites—as long as it was on the waters of the nearby Chesapeake Bay.

"It's none of my business why she's alone," he told himself, stealing peeks at the pretty woman. "She's probably just another brokenhearted soul spending her evenings the best way she can." But Brian couldn't help but watch the customer as she searched the titles for a new mystery to read.

The woman looked to be in her late twenties, just like him. She was tall and slender, with shoulder-length, coal-black hair and bright, clear blue eyes. Brian decided she was a dead ringer for the illustration of the woman on the cover of *Snow White*, complete with rosy cheeks and porcelain skin.

He was studying her from his spot behind the checkout counter in the front of the store when she suddenly looked up from the books and caught him watching her. He smiled self-consciously and quickly began to flip through the papers on his clipboard. Snow White smiled back and returned to her search through the novels.

Brian forced himself to find something else to do besides spy on his customer. Instead he let his mind wander to more personal matters—matters that carried much more weight but were no more haunting. He usually pushed these thoughts from his mind, but now they came back in a rush. Would Michelle come back to him? And, if she did come back, would things be better between them?

Such concerns loomed large for Brian. His ten-month marriage had ended suddenly when his wife, Michelle, walked out on him only two long weeks before. Of course, he'd known his marriage was in trouble; things between them been going steadily downhill for months, but he never dreamed that she'd leave him.

Michelle's unpredictable moods and icy silences had begun shortly after their wedding day, and they baffled him. She'd never displayed mood swings when they were dating, but suddenly nothing he did pleased her. He'd tried coaxing her into talking to him. A nice dinner out at a restaurant worked at first, but then even that failed. "Don't bother me," she'd say. "You can't control me anymore."

Control her? Brian didn't want to control her. He loved her and he wanted to spend the rest of his life with her, but nothing he said or did could convince her of that fact and the situation had gone from bad to worse. The last month they were together was unbearable. Brian found himself losing patience with Michelle's changeable disposition and often grew angry with her. Twice during that month, they'd had ugly, bitter fights, the likes of which he wouldn't have imagined having with anyone, much less the woman he loved. Both fights ended with her storming out of the house and slamming the door behind her. Both times, she'd returned much later, refusing to speak to him for days afterward. He'd even contacted a marriage counselor, but Michelle didn't show up for the appointment.

Brian blinked and rubbed his forehead. Thinking about his wife made him ache all the way to his toes. He went back to watching the woman who looked like Snow White and he wondered if there was someone out there who made her ache inside. He studied her as she scanned the back covers of the mysteries. He liked the way she pushed her dark hair away from her face and the way her forehead wrinkled when she read the jacket of a novel. She was pretty, but there was something else about her that caught his attention and held it. Something that touched him deep inside. He'd been stealing glances at her every Friday night for nearly two months now, and he always came to the same conclusion—Snow White was sad.

There was something about her that seemed fragile, despite the bright smile she always wore. It was as if she'd recently been broken into pieces and had somehow put herself back together again. Brian watched as she pored over the shelves of books, and felt as if he understood exactly what she was going through. He sensed that Snow White's sadness was almost as deep as his own.

Brian was pondering these thoughts when she suddenly glanced up from the shelves of books. Their eyes met again for one fleeting second, and then a smile spread across her pretty face. "I'm sorry," she said, briskly walking to the front of the store carrying a paperback. "You're trying to close up shop, aren't you?"

"No," Brian told her. "We don't close until nine tonight. Take your time. I didn't mean to rush you."

She glanced at her watch and smiled again. "Ten minutes to go. I apologize for taking so long. I lose all track of time when I'm in a bookstore, especially this one. I love this shop."

"Thanks," he said. "I'm the owner and I love it too." He hesitated and then held out his hand. "I'm Brian McKenzie."

"Hi," she said, shaking his hand. "I'm Jenny Sullivan." Her handshake was firmer than many of the men who'd shaken his hand, a fact that led him to the conclusion that Snow White wasn't the shy type after all.

"I've seen you here before," he said. "You certainly love mysteries."

"Guilty," she said, and handed him the paperback she'd so meticulously selected. "Especially the trench coat detective ones. I know they're old fashioned and corny, but I can't get enough of them."

"That's funny; I have many women customers who feel that way about romance novels."

"Not me," she said, wrinkling her nose. "Give me a good mystery and a pepperoni pizza and I'm happy."

"Don't you like romance?" Brian blurted out the sentence before thinking and instantly regretted it.

"Yes," she said, her rosy cheeks turning a deeper shade of pink. "But from what little I remember, romances are for dreamers."

"You're probably right about that," Brian said, and rang up the book on his cash register.

"Don't bother with a bag," she said. "I'll just slip it in my purse."

"Okay," he said and handed her the book. He didn't

want her to go, but could think of no diversion to keep her there. "I put the receipt inside the cover. You can use it as a bookmark. Have a good evening, Jenny. Enjoy your mystery."

"Thanks . . . Brian. It was nice meeting you."

"You too. See you next week."

Chapter Two

Brian closed up the bookstore and then unlocked the bicycle that was chained to the tree near the sidewalk. It was a cool, crisp April night with just a trace of spring hiding in the corners of the chilly darkness. A night that felt exactly the same as the one a few weeks ago when he'd come home and had his final battle with Michelle. As he'd done then, he climbed on his bike and rode through the still busy streets of downtown Annapolis until he arrived at the home they'd purchased six short months ago.

She'd wanted a bigger, newer place in the pricier part of town. Maybe a loft near the harbor or a condo that overlooked the river. But those homes were too expensive for their budget, especially with the bookstore fighting for its life. So they purchased the row house instead. It was small, old and in desperate need of major repairs, but Brian felt certain it would prove

7

itself to be a good investment someday—at least that was what he told Michelle. The truth of the matter was, he'd fallen in love with the place the moment he saw it and he didn't care if they ever made a dime off it.

It was an eighty-year-old row house—a fixer-upper located in the middle of a block in the part of town that could go either way in the next few years. Looking at the house from the street, it appeared as if the interior would be small and narrow. Inside, however, the rooms extended, one after another, deep into the bowels of the house. First, there was the living room, then the dining room, then a study (or a parlor, or a library, or, as Michelle called it, a media room), then, finally, it ended in a galley kitchen.

The kitchen proved to be the biggest hurdle for Michelle to overcome. The appliances were old and often unreliable and the walls were covered with a ghastly lime green flowered wallpaper that was all the rage in the mid-'70s. A door to the back porch opened from the kitchen, but it was a far too dilapidated structure to safely utilize, even just to step outside for a glimpse of the brown, weed-filled backyard.

The upper level of the house was not much better. Instead of the rooms lining up one after another, the upstairs held two ridiculously small bedrooms that lay on either side of a ridiculously narrow hallway. A third bedroom, the master, was at the end of the hall. A room that was somewhat larger and wider than the other bedrooms, but still far too small for Michelle's liking.

"We can add an addition onto the back of the house later," Brian offered.

"Why would we do that?" she asked. "Why not just buy a bigger place? I've had closets bigger than these bedrooms."

It was logic that was tough to argue with, except that they couldn't afford the places where Michelle wanted to buy—not by a long shot—although he understood where she was coming from. Michelle was from a wealthy Baltimore family and it was the first time in her young life she'd been asked to stay within a strict budget. Brian knew it would be a learning experience for both of them. So he sat his wife down and explained to her the facts of life.

First, he told her, the row house was in a good location that was close to their jobs, and while it was true the neighborhood was more than a little seedy, that would change over time. Second, Brian argued, he was handy and could do most of the restoration work himself, saving them untold thousands of dollars. Finally, he pointed out that it was one of the few places in town they could afford, although barely. The house was a bargain—or at least they thought so at the time.

The economic boom of recent years had been good for Annapolis, breathing some much-needed life into the dingier areas of the city. Brian liked the idea of taking the old, forgotten row house and restoring it to its former glory. He thought they were lucky to find the place, even though the real estate market had recently started to stall. Of course, he grossly underestimated the amount of work that was needed, nor could he have known that the value of the houses in the area would begin to decline almost from the moment they'd moved in.

"Don't worry," he told Michelle when the house across the street sold for less than what they'd paid for theirs. "Once we make the repairs, we'll recoup our loss."

But that was six months ago, before the bookstore kept him away from home for twelve hours a day. The real estate market hadn't gotten any better either. Brian took in the view of the neighborhood from his front porch. Another house had a FOR SALE sign in the front yard. It was the third house this month to go on the market. All three had been purchased by young couples over the past year. Couples who'd had the same big plans as Brian. Apparently, the cost and labor involved in the restoration of the houses were beginning to outweigh their charm.

Brian remembered the way the door creaked when he'd walked in that night. "Michelle," he called into the darkened house. "Hey, Baby, I'm home."

Michelle was sitting on the sofa in the front room; a single lamp was lit and the room was dim. She was quietly sipping a glass of white wine and listening to the stereo. Brian was so happy to see her waiting for him that he didn't notice the suitcases stacked up by the front door until after he tried to kiss her cheek. She turned her face away from him. That was when he saw the small overnight bag and the suitcase.

"Hi," he said, his stomach sinking.

"Hi," she said. "My other bags are already in the car. I've been waiting for you. You're late, as usual." He remembered that she was wearing a pair of faded blue jeans and a light blue oxford shirt. But it didn't matter what she wore; Michelle always gave the impression that she'd spent hours selecting her outfit.

"I've been thinking about you all day," he said. The sick feeling in his gut was growing. "I missed you."

"Sit down, Brian," she said. "We have to talk."

He took in a deep breath and blew it out slowly before he sat down next to her. It made his stomach feel slightly better, but it did nothing for his shaking knees. "Michelle," he said, trying to take her hand. "What's going on?"

"I'm not happy," she said with a determined edge in her voice as she pulled her hand from his. "And neither are you. I think it's time we both admitted that our marriage was a mistake. We should never have . . ."

"Our marriage wasn't a mistake!" Brian interrupted, but she shushed him.

"Yes, it was. You know it and I know it. I tried to tell you the way I felt. I tried to tell you I never wanted to live in this house. I tried to tell you I never wanted you to open the bookstore. I wanted you to be a lawyer, Brian. Like me. But you never listened to me."

"Michelle, I . . ."

"No! For once, let me finish saying what I have to say. I've been miserable for months and I don't want to live like this anymore. I should have sat you down and made you listen a long time ago, but I didn't. Instead, I found myself pouting or sulking or crying. For that, I'm sorry."

Brian picked up her hand and squeezed it gently. "Michelle, what are you saying?"

She pulled her hand away again and looked him in

the eye. "We don't want the same things out of life, Brian," she said, with a coolness in her voice that cut through him. "We don't have the same ambitions. We don't have the same dreams. I thought we did, but I was wrong."

"My only ambition is to be with you," he said, finding her hand again.

"Then tell me," she said. "Where do you see us in the future?"

"I see us taking up sailing," he said gently. "We'd get to know the Chesapeake Bay like the back of our hands. You'd be a successful attorney and I'd own a little bookstore in town. We'd fix up the house and have lots of beautiful blond-haired, green-eyed babies."

"That's exactly our problem," Michelle said, prying her hand from his.

"What do you mean? I don't understand."

"Why didn't we ever ask ourselves these questions before, Brian?" she said.

"What do you mean?"

"I mean this." Her hand swept around the living room. "This house, your job . . . I never saw our lives turning out this way, Brian. Not for a minute. This isn't the life I saw for us."

"It's not too late to talk about it," he said. "Tell me now. How did you see our life together?"

She sighed and looked at him accusingly. "I saw us working together, side by side, at your father's firm. We'd be two ambitious attorneys on the way up, rubbing elbows with the movers and shakers of Baltimore. I saw us moving there and opening a branch office of

Hickman, Boris & McKenzie. We'd have to work like dogs, but we'd make the new office every bit as successful as the one in Annapolis. Maybe even more successful. We'd buy a big house in a country club community, and I'd throw elegant dinner parties that would be the talk of the society page. Maybe we'd take up golf, but there would be no sailboats because I get motion sickness, remember? And as for any blond-haired, green-eyed babies . . . Well, maybe there would have been one. Someday! But that wouldn't have been for a long, long time."

"I thought you wanted kids?"

"No," she said, shaking her head. "*You* want kids. *We* never discussed them. *We* never discuss anything. I probably would have agreed to go through with it one time—for your sake—but I don't really like children. They're noisy and messy and they'd ruin my career."

"All right," Brian said. "No kids. Fine. If that's what you want, then . . ."

"Stop!" she said, her voice getting louder. "Kids are not the point."

"What is the point then?"

She flipped back her hair. "Don't you see?" she asked, her eyes steady and cool. "Brian, you've always taken it for granted that anything you wanted was something I wanted too, but you never bothered to ask me whether or not I wanted it."

Her words felt like a slap across his face. "I guess there are a lot of things we should have talked about sooner."

"I guess so," she agreed. "But we didn't, and that's

just as much my fault as yours. We both took it for granted that the other saw things the same way. We never communicated."

"We can start."

"It's too late," she said. "It's better if we end this now. I've already spoken to a lawyer. I'd prefer an annulment over a divorce, but it's too late for that too . . ."

"It's not too late for us!" Brian said. "We can work this out."

"No," Michelle said, and stood up from the sofa. "I'm sorry, Brian," she said, looking down at him. "I don't love you anymore."

"You're just confused right now," he said, standing up and trying to put his arms around her. "We'll go talk to a marriage counselor. We can work through this!"

"I'm not confused," she said, pushing him away. "I know exactly what I'm saying. I don't love you anymore, Brian. I'm sorry if that hurts you, but it's the truth. I don't know if I ever loved you."

Brian sat on the sofa again, feeling as though he'd just been kicked in the stomach.

"I think I was in love with our romance," Michelle was saying, but it sounded as if she was speaking to him from far away. "You do know how to sweep a girl off her feet; I'll say that much for you. But as far as everything else goes . . . A marriage counselor would only be a waste of time for both of us. I've already made up my mind."

"Michelle," Brian said, taking her hand. "You don't mean that . . ."

"Yes, I do," she said. She was standing in front of

him, incredibly beautiful as always, but there was a coolness to her voice he'd never heard before. "I've met someone else," she said, and the words felt like a knife in his chest. "I'm not having an affair," she added. "I would never do that kind of thing. But I won't deny that I have growing feelings for him."

"Who is he?"

"I'm not saying," she said. "But I think he feels the same way. We haven't talked about it, of course, but whenever we're together there's an electricity between us. He takes my breath away, and I can't think about anyone else but him."

"But . . ."

"Not even you," she said, and a teardrop softly spilled down her cheek. "We never had that kind of chemistry, did we?"

Brian sat on the sofa, watching his wife, trying to absorb what she was saying. "I thought we did! Michelle, I love you. Don't do this."

"I'm moving back to Baltimore," she said. "I found another job and I'm starting in two weeks. I think your father would agree that my leaving the firm without the customary notice would be best for everyone."

"I love you!"

"But you never listened to me."

"I'm listening now." He was taken aback by the accusation, mostly because it had the stinging slap of truth to it. He stood up and tried again to wrap his arms around her. "I'm listening now," he repeated,

"Now is too late," she said, her voice sad. "I told you I didn't want to move to this house. I told you I didn't want you to buy the bookstore. But every time I told you how I felt about something, you ignored me."

"I . . . I'm sorry," Brian said. "I'll change. I'll learn how to listen. I'll put whatever you want first. We'll sell the house and . . ."

"It's too late!" Michelle said. She walked to the window and looked out into the dark street for a long time. "I want to be fair," she said, her voice once again chillingly calm. "You can have the house and the bookstore; you were the one who put up the money for the down payments anyway. I'll take the furniture and our savings account. The movers are coming on Monday. You'll have to let them in. I'm sure Luanne will help you refurnish. You never liked my taste anyway."

"Michelle . . ."

"No," she said firmly, holding up her hand to silence him. "My lawyer said I should try to get more out of you, but you know how lawyers are. I told him I didn't want to hurt you. Besides, it would hardly be wise for me to upset your father, would it? So, let's just end this on a friendly note, shall we, Brian?"

"I love you," he said again, and put his arms around her. "You're everything to me. You're my wife and I . . ."

"Don't," she whispered. Then she kissed him, gently at first, and then with a passion he hadn't felt in her for months. "This is for the best," she said at last, breaking away from him. "You'll see."

Then she left, picking up the suitcases as she went and not bothering to shut the door behind her.

"Michelle!" Brian called.

"Don't!" she shouted, as he began to follow her to her car. "I've made up my mind."

"You don't mean that. We can work it out and . . ."

"It's over," she said almost pleadingly as she climbed into her car. "Don't you see that?"

Brian stood stock still and watched her as she drove away, his world crashing around him.

Chapter Three

Ｓhe was there again.

Snow White.

No! It wasn't nice to call her that, especially since Brian was now well aware that her name was Jenny. Jenny Sullivan. He liked the sound of it, and it fit her like a glove.

She was standing in front of the wall of books in the mystery section in deep concentration. She'd already been through all the novels on the two spinning racks and was now closely studying the back flaps of the books on the shelves against the wall.

"Hi, Brian," she'd said when she came into the store that Friday.

"Hi, Jenny."

Brian had seen many people come through the door of his store, but none of them smiled as brightly as Jenny. She smiled from her eyes first and then it spread to her whole face. She was naturally friendly and easy going in a way that made Brian think about his wife. Michelle had a way of sizing people up before she spoke to them. She was always infallibly polite, but she could also be cool and distant. Michelle never smiled first.

Jenny's friendliness baffled Brian. Here was a woman who was open and pleasant, yet, at the same time, there was that ever-present feeling that she was sad, as if someone had hurt her once before. There was something about Jenny's sadness that Brian understood all too well.

Didn't she know how beautiful she was? he wondered. Why wasn't she out on the town on Friday nights, living it up with some lucky guy? Instead, pretty Jenny Sullivan was in his bookstore every Friday, smiling at strangers and looking for a book to take home, preferring the company of a novel and a pepperoni pizza.

Brian tried to occupy his thoughts by studying his clipboard. He reminded himself that it was no sin to enjoy an evening alone—he'd certainly seen his fair share of them lately. Besides, for all he knew, Jenny had a standing date with Prince Charming every Saturday night.

He forced himself to examine the papers on his clipboard. That was certainly a better use of his time than speculating about the love life of a woman he barely knew. He read from the list of titles of newly released books, hoping to make good selections. A brief description of the plot was also provided, but the information was not always helpful. The list changed frequently and often required intensive study in order for Brian to choose which books to order. He made it a habit to keep up with the newspaper and magazine critiques on recently released books, and he spent a good deal of time looking up the authors' names on the Internet. Sometimes his efforts paid off and he was able to glean a few pearls from the multitudes of blockbusters on the list, but it was a time-consuming and thankless process.

Brian scanned the list of books coming out in the mystery genre and wondered what titles would pique the interest of a devoted reader like Jenny Sullivan. He looked up at her and saw that she'd unbuttoned her coat. He tried not to notice the soft curves of her sweater; instead, he blinked his eyes and went back to studying the papers on his clipboard.

He was surprised by the sudden stirring in his gut, and he felt a stab of guilt. He was still a married man, or at least he was for now. Besides, spying on Jenny made him uncomfortable. He hadn't looked at another woman since he'd met Michelle. He hadn't wanted to.

Brian allowed his thoughts to momentarily drift to his wife. She hadn't returned any of his calls. Or the long, heartbroken letter he'd written. He was miserable. He wanted to give Michelle time to think things through, but he also wanted her to come back home. He wasn't sleeping well either.

Lately, he'd been spending his evenings working on the row house. Fortunately, there was plenty of work there to keep him busy. In fact, he considered his to-do list the only thing that was keeping him from going out of his mind.

He missed Michelle.

He was so lost in his thoughts, he didn't notice that Jenny had walked to the front of the store. She was holding a paperback book with a smoking gun on the cover. "Hi," she said.

"Hi," he said, startled. "I didn't hear you walk up."

"I'm sorry. I didn't mean to sneak up on you."

"No," Brian said. "You didn't. I was just going over this list of books. As a matter of fact, you might be able to help me."

"Oh?"

"Yes. I'm going to place my order today."

"That sounds like fun."

"Not hardly. I have to carefully pick the books from this list. I only have so much space on the shelves and I have to make every bit of my inventory count. I need to have the right books on hand. I make my selections mostly from the best sellers list. I also know about the reading assignments for the local high schools and book clubs. But otherwise, I don't have a clue as to what my customers want to read. I need a crystal ball to predict which books will be the most popular. Do you have any suggestions?"

"Sure," she said. "But I can't speak for your other customers. My expertise is only with mysteries, and even there I'm a bit off the beaten path. I think you do need a crystal ball."

"Would you mind taking a look at this list?" Brian asked. "Maybe you can recommend a certain author? Someone that I've missed."

"Of course," she said, taking the clipboard from him. "I have so many favorites . . . Burton Quinn is wonderful, and then there's Frederick Von Suster. He writes the Lady Bromley series. And, of course, Wilson Durban. He's a bit gory, though—definitely not for the squeamish." She flipped through the pages on the clipboard and Brian noticed the way her long, glossy, dark hair fell against the creamy porcelain skin of her face.

"Do you see the section marked 'Genre Fiction—Mystery'?" he asked, leaning over her. She smelled like heaven.

"Uh-huh," she said, her eyes scanning the list. "They don't give you much information about the plot, do they?"

"Just a short blurb."

"Some of the titles sound interesting, but I would have a hard time choosing among them unless I could read the book jacket."

"I research as many of them as I can," Brian said. "Or at least I try to. But there's someone new every week. I could just stick to the big names, but all too often they seem to produce just another version of the book that was written the year before. I want something more for my customers."

"I know what you mean," she said. "That's why I take my time when I look for a book. I want to be surprised by my mysteries. Unfortunately, I usually figure out who the real killer is by the fifth chapter. Aha!"

"Did you find something?"

"Yes," Jenny said. "Right here. Anna Waters! She's wonderful. Her new book is finally being released. It's called *Murder in Orange.*"

"You think that will be a good one?"

"I know I'll buy it," she said. "She lives here, you know."

"Where?"

"Right here in Annapolis."

"Who?"

"Anna Waters. That's not her real name, of course. Her real name is Maggie Monson. The 'Anna' is short for Annapolis and the 'Waters' is for the Severne River that flows close to her home."

"I never knew there was a mystery writer right here in our midst."

"She keeps a low profile," Jenny said. "And Maggie Monson isn't just any mystery writer. She's a fascinating person. She was a nurse, a newspaper reporter, a school teacher, a dog groomer . . . oh, and a truck driver for a company that manufactures children's shoes. She's raised five children and she's a grandmother to four more. She's also active in the Save The Bay Foundation. Oh, and her husband is an attorney in town."

"Is his name Frank Monson, by any chance?"

"Yes. That's him. Do you know him?"

"I've met him a few times. He specializes in contract law, right?"

"I don't know," Jenny said. "Anna told me his specialty was ambulance chasing, but I think she was only kidding. You never know with Anna."

"She sounds like a nut," Brian said.

"You could say that, I guess. But she's also an incredible writer. I almost never know how her mysteries will end—and I'm good at figuring out the endings. She writes the Bux McGee series. They're the best mysteries I've ever read, and I'm not just saying that because I know the author. Once you pick up a Bux McGee book, you won't put it down. You should meet her."

"I'd like that," Brian said.

"Really? Because I might be able to arrange it."

"Sure. I love meeting writers."

"Wonderful," Jenny exclaimed. "I'll tell her about you and your store—if you'd like me to, that is?"

"That would be great. Maybe we could arrange for a book signing . . . if you think she'd be interested. She does do signings, doesn't she?"

"I don't know," Jenny said. "Maybe. I met her at the library last year when she was doing a reading from *Murder in Pink* and speaking about her experiences as a mystery writer. *Murder in Pink* was the first book in the series. It was about Bux solving the murder of a ballerina. Of course, he fell in love with the prime suspect—another ballerina. I won't tell you how it ends; you'll have to read it for yourself. Next came *Murder in White*. That was where the victim was found murdered on her wedding night, still in her white gown. Of course, you think it's the groom who did it, but . . . Never mind. You'll have to read that one too."

"I will."

"*Murder in Orange* is the third book in the series, and

I bet it will be the best one yet. I meet Anna for lunch every week or so. I'll tell her about you the next time I see her. I don't want to speak for her, of course, but she might be open to doing a signing here. She likes to take walks downtown and she likes to read. I'll ask her to stop by here the next time she's in the neighborhood."

"That would be great," Brian said, and he meant it. He hadn't done a book signing before, and he was open to anything that would bring some more foot-traffic through the door.

Jenny smiled ear to ear. "This could be a lot of fun," she said.

"Thanks," he said. "I'd appreciate it if you talked to Ms. Waters. And I'll be sure to order a big batch of her books."

Chapter Four

Brian met Michelle Wellman two years ago at his father's law firm. He was spending his last summer of law school working as an intern for the firm of Hickman, Boris & McKenzie, located in the heart of downtown Annapolis.

Annapolis, Maryland, while not on the same level as New York City or Los Angeles, or even nearby Baltimore, was still the state capital and also a city of influence. The law firm of Hickman, Boris & McKenzie was at the heart of that influence. The firm's client roster included many Maryland State lawmakers, business leaders, and top brass from the Naval Academy. It also enjoyed considerable business and political muscle.

Brian's father, Simon McKenzie, was a founding member of the firm—a fact that often made Brian feel as if it required an explanation. Being the boss's son weighed heavily on him, and he worked hard to prove to his coworkers and clients that he was every bit as capable an attorney as anyone else in the firm. He immersed himself completely in his work, consistently working more hours than anyone else, including his father.

Michelle worked at the firm, as well. She began as an intern during her last semester at the University of Maryland and was commuting from Baltimore. She'd wanted to work closer to her home city, but the offer to work for the prestigious Hickman, Boris & McKenzie was too good an opportunity to pass up.

She was the most beautiful woman Brian had ever seen. She was so beautiful, his father hesitated in hiring her. "Too pretty," he grumbled. "None of the other interns will get any work done because they'll be too busy looking at her." But her resumé was impressive, as was everything about Michelle.

She was tall, with long, straight, blond hair that hung down her back and swung softly when she walked. Her skin was flawless and her cheeks always had a pretty pink glow to them. Her mouth was shaped like a small, perfect bow and her small teeth were as white as snow. Her eyes were an incredible shade of jade green and she had impossibly long eyelashes. Her body was slim and lean, with soft curves in all the right places and nine miles of leg.

"Hi," Brian said, as a million needles and pins swept over him. "I'm Brian McKenzie."

"McKenzie?" she said. "Are you any relation to Simon McKenzie?"

"Yes," Brian winced. "He's my father, but . . ." His words trailed off. What could he say? "Yes, the boss is my old man and yes, he gave me a job, but I work as hard as anyone else." Or maybe he could have said, "I know you've heard my father is a pitbull in the courtroom, but he isn't like that at home. Underneath that brash exterior beats the heart of a big teddy bear."

Simon McKenzie was a legend in the legal community of Annapolis. An ambitious, sometimes ruthless man, he was the lawyer-of-choice for the high and mighty in Annapolis. His name regularly appeared on the front page of the newspaper. He dined with presidents and royalty and had even shaken hands with the Pope. Of course, few people knew that Simon liked to spend his free time on a sailboat in the Chesapeake Bay, or checking his crab traps (in season, of course), or taking orders from his tiny but endlessly energetic wife, Luanne.

Simon McKenzie had always taken for granted that Brian would choose law as a career path. And why not? He loved being an attorney and he loved the life that went along with it. Rubbing elbows with power brokers came easily to this confident and gregarious man. It was always assumed that his children would feel the same way. He was shocked when Brian told him in his senior year of high school that he wanted to teach. Or open a bookstore.

"Nonsense," Simon said. "You're only seventeen. You're still wet behind the ears. You don't know what you want to do with your life yet. I think we should stick with the original plan. You'll study pre-law with a strong business curriculum and then you'll go on to law school. A few summers working at the firm will put that fire in your belly."

Brian believed him. Simon had always taken it for granted that his children would follow in his footsteps, and so far he'd been correct in that assumption. Brian's sister, Natalie, was currently working for the District Attorney's office, and his brother Ted had a small but growing practice in Columbia. So Brian studied pre-law with a strong business curriculum and then he went on to law school. His grades were excellent and he belonged to all the right clubs and fraternities. Meanwhile, he waited to feel the "fire in his belly" his father spoke of—but it never came. Of course, after meeting Michelle, a career as an attorney sounded better than ever.

He fell in love with her on their first date. They went to a quiet little place around the corner from the office, and drinks turned into dinner and then into a walk around the harbor. It was a warm night in June, but the feel of her small hand inside of his sent shivers all the way to his toes.

On their second date, they went to the zoo. The day after that they went to a play in Baltimore. The next day, they went to Brian's favorite Italian restaurant. The day after that, they went out for sushi. She took him to art museums and antique shows. He took her hiking and fishing.

His father quickly figured out the reason for his son's sudden dazed expression at work, and extended a dinner invitation to the young couple. Of course, Brian was horrified by the thought and avoided it for as long as possible, right up until his mother threatened him with bodily harm.

"What are you afraid of?" Luanne McKenzie asked. "I won't bite her."

"That's what you said last time," Brian said.

"I barely broke the skin."

"I know, Mom. But I don't want to rush her. This one's special."

After three months, however, Michelle suggested a meeting. "When do I get to meet your folks?" she asked.

"You already know my dad."

"You've told me so much about your mother," she said. "I'd like to meet her too."

"I'll set it up," Brian said hesitantly, and he did. A cookout was arranged at the McKenzie homestead.

They arrived a half-hour late—an offense that was sure to annoy Brian's punctual father, but try explaining that to Michelle on a bad hair day. Fortunately, Simon didn't notice their tardiness and greeted them warmly. "Come in," he boomed, slapping Brian on the back and giving Michelle a bear hug that almost knocked her off her feet. "It's great you kids are here!"

"Thank you, Mr. McKenzie," Michelle said. He was, after all, her boss.

"Now, Michelle. We're not in the office. Please, call me Simon."

"Simon."

He led them into the backyard, where Luanne was sitting at a picnic table in the shade of a maple tree. At her feet was Huckleberry, the family's ten-year-old, yellow Labrador Retriever.

"Hello," Luanne said, jumping to her feet and coming toward them.

But then something happened that would greatly trouble Brian's mother in the months ahead. An occurrence which she'd later see as a sign of bad tidings. It would come to be known as "The Huckleberry Incident."

Huckleberry growled.

At first it was a low, barely audible noise coming from the old dog. As if he was grumbling about being disturbed from his afternoon nap. But the growl grew louder and longer and more unfriendly.

"Huckleberry!" Brian scolded. "Knock it off!" But Huckleberry was not listening. Instead, his growl rumbled deeper until it became an irritated yelp.

"Does he bite?" Michelle asked, standing stock still.

"No," Brian's mother said. "Huckleberry, you be nice. He's usually such a mellow dog."

But Huckleberry was anything but mellow. He was on his feet and barking; his long tail stood erect and quivered in indignation. The hair on his back stood on end as he took a step closer to Michelle.

"Get him away from me!" she said, petrified.

"I'll take him inside," Brian said, grabbing hold of Huckleberry's collar. "What's gotten into you, you old bird dog? Bad boy!" He dragged the reluctant dog into the house, chastising him the whole way.

"I'm sorry, dear," Luanne McKenzie said, baffled. "I've never seen him like this."

"I thought he was going to bite me," Michelle said, still shaken.

"No," Luanne scoffed. "Huckleberry is as old as the hills and he wouldn't hurt a fly. We must have woken him up from a very deep sleep. He's never acted this way before."

But Huckleberry had frightened Michelle to the point of terror, and she still looked fearful. "That dog is mean," she said with a shudder.

Luanne McKenzie was taken aback by Michelle's accusation. "Mean?" she said. "Huckleberry isn't mean. He's the best dog I've ever had."

Michelle looked at Luanne as if she'd lost her mind. "I guess I'm not a dog person," she said at last.

"I'm sorry he frightened you," Luanne said. "But he really isn't mean."

"Now, Lu," Simon said. "You can hardly blame Michelle for her concern. Huckleberry's behavior here today has been atrocious. Michelle, please accept our humble apologies. Our dog is getting old and ill-tempered."

"Yes," Luanne said, handing Michelle a glass of iced tea. "Don't worry about him, dear. We'll keep him inside for the rest of the evening."

"Thank you," Michelle said, relaxing somewhat as she accepted the glass.

Luanne smiled at Michelle but still felt somewhat ill at ease. It wasn't like Huckleberry to take such an instant dislike to a visitor. He was usually such a friendly dog. She studied the young woman thoughtfully. She looked okay enough, Luanne told herself. But still . . . If it was any other dog but Huckleberry. He always seemed to know which people to attach himself to and which to steer clear from. And he'd never barked like that at anyone else.

"I put him in the laundry room," Brian said, returning from the house. "He was already starting to fall asleep by the time I shut the door. He's getting to be an old man, isn't he?"

Luanne's apprehensions about Michelle melted away as soon as she saw the way Brian slipped his arms around her and smiled sweetly into her face.

"All better?" he asked, his voice soft and low.

"All better," she said, smiling up at him.

Luanne shook off her reservations. How could she not like this woman when Brian was so clearly smitten?

"I hope everyone's hungry," Simon said. "Brian, would you be so kind as to set the table while I man the grill? These burgers won't cook themselves, you know. Luanne, I think we can bring out the salad now."

"You have a lovely home, Mrs. McKenzie," Michelle said once they were all seated around the patio table.

"Why, thank you," Luanne said. "We've been here for almost one hundred years now, right, Simon?"

"Right, my beloved," Simon said. "But don't forget to tell Michelle that it was you who made our modest home the palace that it is today."

Luanne smiled. "The palace needs a new roof," she said. "And a little paint wouldn't hurt either."

Brian just rolled his eyes at Michelle. It was a conversation that occurred whenever company came around. Someone would compliment Luanne on her home, and she would then shoo away the comment like a bothersome bee. But the McKenzie home was indeed lovely, and that fact was clear to anyone and everyone who entered.

Brian explained to Michelle how his family had purchased the two-acre lot of Annapolis waterfront real estate almost twenty-five years ago. Back when land was not nearly so expensive and back when Simon McKenzie had just begun practicing law. It took several years to build the house—or at least the original house. The addition came later, as did the guest house, swimming pool, patio, gazebo, boathouse and dock that led to the family's sailboat. The McKenzies lived in a trailer on the land until the lot was paid for and the house was built—a cramped seven years for the growing brood.

Luanne McKenzie handled all the construction details while her husband built his law practice. She personally hired the architects, carpenters, electricians, plumbers, and other assorted contractors to see that the work was completed to her liking. When it was possible, she'd do the job herself. She left no detail to chance. Materials were paid for as the family could afford them and not a moment sooner. From lumber to paint to grass seed, nothing was purchased on credit.

Brian told Michelle that his first memories were of scaffolding and drywall and watching his mother swing a hammer from his perch by the window of the little trailer. Even after the house was finally erected, there were endless projects and renovations. In fact, he couldn't remember a single time in his life when his mother was not working on some extensive project or another around the house. From landscaping to painting to laying the stone patio, Luanne McKenzie didn't mind getting her hands dirty. In fact, she enjoyed it. Family folklore told of the day when Luanne spent the morning on a ladder hanging wallpaper in the kitchen and the afternoon giving birth to Natalie.

When Brian and his siblings were old enough, they were recruited as helpers. Luanne was uncompromising in her standards, even for her children, and Brian's workmanship rivaled that of a seasoned carpenter by the time he was out of grade school. He liked working for his mother almost as much as he liked lying in a hammock on a hot summer day, reading books one after another.

Michelle assumed that Luanne McKenzie acted as an overseer of the estate—a sort of Martha Stewart for the Chesapeake Bay—but Brian said no. "Not so," he told her. "Most people don't realize that the wife of the legendary Simon McKenzie was ready, willing and able to shimmy up on the roof to patch a leak or take apart the porch steps only to put them back up again on the opposite side—all the while cussing like a sailor." A statement which was an exaggeration, but not by much.

"I learned to hammer a nail without bending it before I was three," Brian told her.

"Why didn't she just hire someone?" Michelle asked. A remark he found adorable.

"What's the fun in that?" he said, knowing that explaining the behavior of his mother to someone who didn't know her was an impossible task.

"More iced tea?" Luanne asked.

"Yes, please," Michelle said. "Your garden is lovely."

"Thank you. I don't have nearly enough time to keep up with the weeds, but you caught us on a good day. Do you like to garden?"

Michelle looked at her, puzzled for a moment. "Why, um . . . I'm not sure. I've never tried it. Law school and work haven't left much room for gardening."

"Perhaps one day Brian will show you some gardening basics—just in case you want to grow something."

"We're keeping Michelle much too busy at work for her to take up gardening, Poopsie," Simon told his wife. "Brian, as well, would be hard pressed to find the time."

"It's true," Brian echoed. "As much as I would like that. Besides, Mom, Michelle lives in a small apartment in Baltimore. She doesn't have much of a homestead."

Luanne smiled but, secretly, she saw Michelle's lack of gardening skills as further evidence of a dubious character. "How do you like your apartment?" she asked. "Baltimore is such a lovely city."

"I like living in Baltimore. I grew up there. I love the hustle and bustle of it. Of course, I spend a good deal of my time commuting. It's only thirty miles to Annapolis, but the traffic can be a horror."

His mother nodded again. "Well, now that you're out of law school and working for the firm, I'm sure you'll find a nice apartment right here in Annapolis."

"Maybe. There are some nice places in town, but I'd miss Baltimore. Everyone I know is there."

Michelle looked uncomfortable so Brian stepped in.

"Mom," he said. "Stop picking on her. Michelle likes it where she is now."

"I'm not picking on her," Luanne said. "It was simply a suggestion."

"Thank you," he said. "I'm sure she'll take it under advisement."

His mother gave him a warning look, then shot Michelle a big smile. The rest of the evening went without further incident. As a matter of fact, it turned into a pleasant evening for everyone.

"She's lovely, honey," Luanne whispered to her son later that night. "Simply lovely."

Chapter Five

"Are you Brian McKenzie?" the woman in the tan trench coat asked.

"Yes," he said. It was an overcast, rainy day that matched his mood to a T. Brian was standing behind the counter of his bookstore when the woman walked in. He'd just taken a sip from his coffee cup, only to realize it had grown cold. "May I help you?"

"My name is Maggie Monson," she said. "But you can call me Anna Waters. Jenny Sullivan suggested I drop by and meet you. I was in the neighborhood so I thought I'd pop in. This is a lovely shop. So much more intimate than one of the chain stores."

"Thank you," Brian said, coming out from behind the counter and shaking her hand vigorously. "Jenny's told me about you. I'm glad to meet you, Mrs. Waters . . . Or would you prefer that I call you by your given name?"

"Anna will do," she said.

"Anna. Thank you for coming by. I just finished *Murder in Pink* and I've got to tell you, I loved it! I'm not much of a mystery fan, but I couldn't put it down."

"What, then?" she asked.

"I beg your pardon?"

"What, then, do you read?" she asked again.

"Oh," he said. "Um . . . just about anything, I guess. I like historical fiction, particularly from the World War II era. I also read the classics, although I prefer American authors. And I try to keep up with the best-sellers list. Basically, Anna, I try to read whatever my customers are reading."

"And how's that working for you?"

"It's hit or miss," he confessed. "Some months I know what the next big thing will be, and I have it on my shelves when someone comes in looking for it. Some months, I don't."

She grinned at him. "Maybe you're trying too hard to make people happy."

"Maybe. But that's my job."

Anna Waters was a curiosity. In addition to the battered trench coat, she wore a wilted navy blue canvas hat and knee-high black-rubber rain boots, all of which had seen better days. When she removed the dripping hat, Brian saw her curly red hair and bright green eyes. She was a wet, rumpled woman but there was something about her that seemed familiar. A glint to her eye and an energy in her step. It would be days before Brian realized that Anna Waters reminded him of his mother. Why, he didn't know, because there was little physical

resemblance other than their ages, but there was something about Anna's straightforward, no-nonsense man-
ner that came from the same mold as the one used to
make Luanne McKenzie.

"Just how many books have you written?" Brian
asked. "I'd like to have at least one copy of each on
hand at the store before the book signing."

"Oh, my," Anna said, frowning. "I don't count
them!"

"You don't?"

"Heavens, no. I wouldn't dream of it. That would be
ludicrous. I just keep writing them and my publisher
keeps publishing them. I usually write two or three at
the same time."

"Doesn't that get confusing?"

"No. It works out quite well, actually. Usually, by the
time I'm putting down the bones of one story, another
story pops into my head. By the time I've developed it
to the point where I'm ready to put it on paper, the first
story is ready to be edited. Of course, I usually get to a
point where I have to set one story aside in order to
complete the other. But the process isn't as difficult as
you would think. I think I'm averaging two or three
books a year."

"That's remarkable," Brian said. "You're quite pro-
lific. How long have you been writing?"

"Ever since I was a born, it seems, but I never published anything until about seven years ago. I wrote *A
Chesapeake Murder* while my husband was away on a
business trip and my youngest two children were off at
college. I wrote it in six days and sent it to a New York

City literary agent I saw on a TV show. It was in print a year later. I've been writing ever since."

"You're kidding?" Brian asked, shocked.

"No, sir," she said, looking puzzled. "Why would I kid you?"

"I'm sorry," he said. "I didn't mean to insult you. It's just that I've heard that it's difficult to break into publishing. I don't often hear of a writer writing a book in six days and then selling it to the first person she sends it to."

She shrugged. "I got lucky, I guess, and they haven't all been that easy. Now, to discuss the possibility of a book signing, you should know that I only do them every now and then. I don't particularly care for sitting at a table waiting for people to approach me. You should also know that I may periodically feel compelled to walk about the store and mingle with the customers. I like meeting my fans and I find it makes for a more pleasurable experience. Don't you agree?"

"Yes."

"Additionally, I don't care one way or the other if I sell a single book, so don't expect miracles. I've developed a loyal, albeit offbeat, following. The revenues generated from my novels are not extensive, but they keep me comfortable. And I'm comfortable with comfortable."

Brian smiled. Clearly, Anna Waters was as colorful a character as any that graced the pages of her novels. "I would personally be more comfortable with selling lots of books," he said with a wry smile. "But if you're comfortable, I'm comfortable."

"Then we've reached an agreement, young man."

"Good. I'll see to it that a press release goes out so your loyal readers will know all the pertinent information. Would next month be convenient?"

"Saturday, July 10," she said.

"That would be fine," Brian said. "I can send over an agreement for you to sign."

"You must have a background in law," she said.

"Yes," he said. "As a matter of fact, I am . . . I was . . . a lawyer. In fact, I've met your husband, Frank."

"Is that so?" she said, her eyebrows shooting up. "May I ask you a question, Mr. McKenzie?"

"Of course."

"During your career as an attorney, you weren't, by any chance, affiliated with the firm of Hickman, Boris & McKenzie?"

"Yes." Brian sighed, waiting for the inevitable question.

"Are you related to Simon McKenzie?"

"Yes. He's my father."

"Delightful," Anna said. "You must be the wayward son I've heard tell of."

"Yes, that would be me."

"Congratulations!" she said and slapped him hard on the back. "It's about time someone told that old son-of-a-gun, Simon McKenzie, that there's more to life than the practice of law."

"Do you know my father?"

"No. We've never had the pleasure of being formally introduced, but my husband speaks highly of him.

Frank tells me he'd have loved to have seen the look on your father's face when his son told him he wanted to blaze his own trail. Bully for you, young man! Bully for you!"

"Thank you," Brian said. "I think. But my father is convinced that I'm going to come to my senses any day now and return to the firm. He keeps reminding me that I'm still a member in good standing of the Maryland State Bar Association."

Anna Waters smiled again; it was a crazy, maniacal kind of smile that Brian couldn't decipher. "I won't hold that against you," she said, shaking his hand with the force of a gorilla. "Tell your father that Frank Monson sends his best."

"I will."

"Have a nice day."

"Wait," Brian said, as she swung open the door. "How do I get hold of you?"

"You can reach me through Jenny Sullivan," Anna said. "You're her friend, correct?"

"She's a customer."

"And she's a peach of a girl. Just send a message through Jenny if you need to reach me, Mr. Bookstore Owner/Lawyer. And, as far as a written contract spelling out the terms of our agreement, a handshake is all I need. We're golden."

With that she was gone in a flash. Brian watched Anna Waters through the window as she made her way down the street. It was pouring and she had no umbrella, only the soggy raincoat and hat. But she didn't seem to mind the weather as she bounded full-speed down the sidewalk. There was a nothing-but-business charge in her step, and she was oblivious to the pelting rain coming down on her.

Chapter Six

"Are you sure about this?" Luanne McKenzie asked Brian a year ago, when he told her that he was going to ask Michelle to marry him.

"What do you mean?" Brian said. "Michelle's perfect. Anyone can see that just by looking at her. She's beautiful and intelligent and . . . Well, Dad likes her, at least. And, for your information, Michelle certainly thinks the world of you. What's the problem, Mom?"

"Nothing," she said. "It's nothing! It's just that Huckleberry . . ."

"Huckleberry?"

"Yes, Huckleberry."

"Huckleberry's a dog!"

"I noticed that too. But Huckleberry's always been an excellent judge of character and he has considerable reservations about Michelle."

"I can't believe this," Brian groaned. "Could it be

that Michelle and I simply caught Huckleberry on a bad day? If you remember, he was sleeping when we walked into the yard. Maybe we woke him up or maybe he didn't like her perfume."

"His reaction is the same every time he sees her! He doesn't like her, Brian. He's made himself quite clear on that point."

"Huckleberry's getting old. Besides, you certainly can't blame Michelle because our dog doesn't like her. Are you sure it isn't you who has reservations?"

"Of course not!" Luanne said. "I adore Michelle. It's just that marriage is such an important step. You haven't known her for long . . . and you're both so gosh-darned young."

"I'm twenty-six," he said. "And I've known Michelle long enough to know that I love her and I want to spend the rest of my life with her."

Brian was surprised by his mother's reaction to what he thought was happy news. He'd sensed his mother's qualms about Michelle and while he hadn't expected her to kick up her heels for joy, he hadn't expected the look of horror on her face either.

"There's twenty-six," his mother said. "And then there's twenty-six. You and Michelle are still wet behind the ears. Did you write the prenuptial agreement yet?"

"We don't need one. And, for your information, I'm old enough to decide if I'm ready for marriage. I love her, Mom, and it would be nice if you liked her too. She doesn't garden or reupholster furniture or even know how to steam a pot of crabs, but she's smart and beautiful and wonderful in every way I can see. And you, of all people, should be happy for us!"

Luanne McKenzie was taken aback by Brian's sudden defensiveness. Not that she didn't like an argument every now and then. Good heavens, no! Living in a house full of lawyers would sharpen anyone's debating skills, and no McKenzie ever backed down from a dispute, large or small. But she could see by the stubborn tightening of Brian's jaw and the cool glint in his eye that he was ready to go toe-to-toe in defense of Michelle's virtues. Virtues Luanne had never been able to distinguish. So, she wisely pasted a smile on her face. "You've made your case quite clear, son," she told him. "And that's all I needed to hear. Michelle will make a sweetheart of a daughter-in-law and I'm as pleased as punch to welcome her to the family."

It was hard to choke out the words and Luanne suspected she had not fooled her son one iota. But she'd learned long ago that arguing with her middle child (or any other member of her family) was like wrestling with a greased pig—it was best to come prepared and wear good boots. She also got the acute impression that there was nothing she could say to Brian that would make him change his mind. Obviously, the Huckleberry argument was not persuasive enough to sway his decision. In the end, the simple truth of the matter was that Luanne didn't have enough evidence to support her charges against Michelle. It was more of a gut feeling anyway but, unfortunately, gut feelings didn't hold up well in court.

"She's too pretty for you, Lu," Simon said. "Let her

give birth to a couple of kids and age a decade or two. She'll ugly up nicely. You'll like her better then. Trust Brian. He's head-over-heels for this gal and he's always been a level-headed kid. He knows what he wants."

Luanne tried to keep her opinions to herself. What good would it do to voice unfounded reservations about her soon-to-be daughter-in-law? Neither Brian nor Simon had much patience for unfounded suspicions. In fact, most McKenzies preferred complaints to be spelled out clearly, preferably in black and white and in triplicate. Just the facts, thank you. All Luanne could do was hope that Brian would come to his senses.

Of course, he didn't, and six months after they met, Brian proposed to Michelle. Four months later they took their vows in the McKenzies' backyard gazebo over-looking the water. It was a beautiful wedding with a hundred guests. Simon paid for the whole thing as a gift to the newlyweds. They honeymooned at the Delaware shore. After they returned, they moved into the row house, an arrangement Luanne suspected Michelle saw as temporary.

Brian saw the house as a diamond in the rough, but Luanne could tell that Michelle saw it as a dilapidated, ugly hole in the wall located in a part of town she'd have been reluctant to drive through, much less live in. Brian paid the down payment and closing costs from his savings. He had lived with his parents up until the time he married, and had accumulated a respectable amount of money. After the newlyweds moved in, Brian used the same methods of home repair he'd seen his mother make over the years. Tackle one project at a time, do it exceedingly well, then move on to the next. Michelle wanted the house renovated quickly . . . so they could sell it and move. She was appalled when she realized that her new husband intended to make most of the repairs himself and was in no particular hurry to finish.

Three months after they moved in, the outside of the house had been painted, the crumbling cement sidewalk had been replaced with a brick one, and a fresh coat of paint had been given to all the interior rooms—all in the cool shades of gray that Michelle was strangely drawn to.

"We should sell now," Michelle would complain to Luanne on the rare occasions when they came by to visit. "We'll be lucky to break even with our investment and Brian hasn't even touched the kitchen yet. Or the bathrooms."

"It's coming along great," Brian would tell Luanne, as if his wife's comments were the most adorable thing he'd ever heard. "This is the fun part." Michelle would shudder and grit her teeth and Luanne saw what her son refused to see—Michelle was not having fun.

Chapter Seven

Jenny Sullivan walked into the bookstore on Friday night as if on cue.

"Hi," Brian said, grinning. It felt strange to grin, it had been so long, but the sight of Jenny made him smile.

"Hey, there," she said, smiling back. "I hear Anna stopped by."

"Yes," he said. "We're having the book signing on July 10. I've already called the newspaper and I'm making some fliers on my computer to put in the window and in the shops around town."

"You'll be surprised by how many people show up," she said. "Anna doesn't make public appearances often. She's a bit of a J. D. Salinger."

"She did seem a bit eccentric."

"Not so much," Jenny said. "She's just straightforward and she doesn't suffer fools. There isn't an ounce

50

of pretense in her whole body. Anna disdains any form of phoniness and has little use for people who are not as quick-witted as she is. Do you know the type of person I mean?"

"Painfully, I'm afraid."

Jenny smiled again. "There's a story behind that remark, but I won't ask."

"Thanks. Her new novel just came in." Brian pulled a hardcover book with an orange paper jacket out from behind the counter. "I've ordered four of them, and three already sold. I saved this one for you. Nice artwork on the cover."

"Thank you so much!" Jenny accepted the book with an expression of delight. "This is my lucky day. I've been waiting for this for over six months." She pulled out her wallet, but Brian waved it away.

"This one's on me," he said. "I had no idea who Anna Waters was until you told me. Apparently, she has a very loyal following. I'm surprised none of my customers asked me to order her books sooner."

"Most of the chains don't know who she is either. Her fans are used to ordering her books over the Internet. That's what I do."

"Ouch," Brian said. "You sure know how to hurt a guy."

"Sorry. I'll never do it again."

"I'd appreciate that."

"No problem."

She smiled again and took the book he handed her. "Well," she said, almost reluctantly. "My pepperoni pizza awaits."

"Does your husband work late on Fridays?" Brian blurted out the question before thinking it through, and as soon as he said it, he regretted it.

"I'm not married." She said with a sheepish smile.

"Boyfriend?"

Jenny raised her eyebrows and gave him an expression of mock surprise.

"I'm not usually this forward. It's just that I see you here every Friday and I couldn't help but wonder . . ."

"I know, I know," she said, folding her arms stubbornly over her chest. "What's a nice girl like me doing in a bookstore on a Friday night? You and my father should meet. You seem to have a lot in common."

"I apologize for being pushy. I'm not usually this obnoxious. I was curious about things that are none of my business. I'm sorry."

"That's all right," Jenny said. "I get that a lot. To tell you the truth, I haven't met the right guy yet and, for now at least, I like my Friday nights just the way they are."

Brian didn't ask for more details. He could have kicked himself for getting personal with his pretty customer. All the same, he was glad he knew more about her. And he was glad to hear she was unattached. "Do you work around here?" he said, changing the subject.

"Yes," Jenny said. "By day, I'm a draftsman—or rather, a draftswoman—with Fuller & Kline. They're an architect firm downtown. They design mostly schools, sometimes office buildings."

"I've heard of them."

"I've been there about five years. I'm thinking about cutting my hours back, though. I'm finding it difficult keeping up with my second job."

"Oh, what's your second job?"

"I paint," she said. "Mostly paintings of the Bay."

"I'd love to see your work," Brian said, and meant it. "I bet you're a good painter. Do you paint with oils or water colors?"

"I'm not that kind of painter, although I have done some watercolors for a few of my special clients. My specialty, however, is painting furniture and walls."

"Really?" he asked. "I've done some furniture refinishing work myself."

"I don't refinish the furniture. I just paint on it. You know, flowers, grape leaves, lighthouses. That sort of thing. Sometimes I paint murals."

"Oh, like decoupage?"

"Sort of, except I paint freehand."

"Hmm," Brian said. "I'd like to see your work. It sounds as if you're a busy lady. When do you find time to read all your mysteries?"

"Friday nights are all mine."

"My mother could use your help. She has an old cedar chest she keeps painting over and over again. One week it's white, the next week it's stripped down to bare wood."

"Here's my card," she said, pulling a little blue card from her purse. *Jenny's Faux Fun*, it read, along with some doodled flowers and a phone number.

"Thanks," Brian said. "But I must warn you. My mother makes Anna Waters look shy and retiring."

"I like her already," Jenny said. Then she picked up her book, gave him another heart-stopping smile and walked out the door.

Chapter Eight

Brian's decision to quit his job at his father's law firm and open the bookstore hadn't come easy but, once the process was set in motion, he was sure he'd made the right choice and there was no turning back.

"Why would you want to open a bookstore?" his father asked. "What kind of lawyer has a bookstore? The firm has a perfectly fine law library, Brian. It doesn't make sense. I've never heard of such a thing!"

"It's something I've always wanted to do, Pop," Brian said.

"And what does your wife say about this?"

"She thinks I'm crazy, but Michelle's the reason I feel like I'm ready to take the plunge."

"Why's that?"

"Because," Brian said, adamantly. "My life's great now that I'm with Michelle. She's perfect and I'm happier than I've ever been in my life, except for one thing. Do you want to know what that one thing is?"

"I'm afraid to ask."

"Pop, I don't want to be a lawyer."

"But you're good at it," Simon argued. "You're smart and detailed and passionate about your clients. You're an excellent lawyer, Brian, and I'm not saying that because you're my son. I've never had a single complaint about any of the work you've done for the firm. You put in more hours than anyone else and . . ."

"I'm not happy doing it, Pop," Brian interrupted. "In fact, I'm miserable."

"Miserable?" Simon was baffled. He couldn't understand how it could be that his own son didn't love practicing law as much as he did.

"It works for you," Brian added. "And it works for Ted and Natalie and Michelle."

"Michelle isn't half the lawyer you are," Simon blurted out, then thought better of the statement. "Don't get me wrong. Michelle is . . . good at what she does but, Brian, you're brilliant at it! Brilliant."

"Thank you," Brian said. "But, my brilliance aside, I'm not happy doing what I'm doing and I can't imagine waking up day after day, year after year, to do a job that makes me unhappy. Look, Pop, I'm going to tell you what I told Michelle—I want to give this bookstore a fair chance. If it doesn't work out, I can always go back to practicing law. Right?"

"We're McKenzies," Simon argued. "McKenzies have great hair and poor eyesight after the age of thirty-five. We're also tall and have unusually sweaty feet and, most importantly, McKenzies are lawyers. It's almost a Maryland state law. Didn't you get the memo?"

Eventually, however, Simon came around. As did Brian's mother, brother, and sister. Everyone came around that is, except for Michelle. She proved to be the biggest holdout to bless Brian's decision. She cried. She pleaded. She argued. She shouted.

"This is unacceptable!" she said. "You graduated from Loyola at the top of your class! You're from a family of lawyers! Your father is a founding partner of the firm! You could be running the place in a few years, Brian. Why would you want to throw all that away to open a musty, smelly, old bookstore?"

"Because my life is perfect since I met you," he told her. "I'm in love and everything has fallen into place just the way I'd always hoped it would. Except for one thing—I hate my job. Michelle, I became a lawyer because it was expected of me. I'm a McKenzie, after all."

"Exactly!"

"But that's precisely why I don't want to be a lawyer."

"I don't understand," she said. "I was hoping we would talk your father into letting us open up a satellite office in Baltimore next year. We could sell the row house and move there and then we could . . ."

Brian looked at her, confused. This was all new information to him. "I don't want to be a lawyer, and I thought you liked living in Annapolis."

"I do," she said, swallowing. "But Baltimore is great too. You'd love it there and we could buy a nice place near the inner harbor and . . ."

"Let's try this first," he said. "If it doesn't work out, we'll do it your way."

"When?" Michelle asked. "Don't make promises you can't keep, Brian. I've given up so much already!"

The remark caught him off-guard. He knew Michelle was not one hundred percent behind him with respect to the decisions they'd made as husband and wife, but she understood the reasons and knew their logic had been sound.

Later, Brian realized this would be the first sign that Michelle was less than happy in their marriage. He pressed her to explain what she meant. He wanted to know what it was she felt that she'd given up, but she never did say. Of course he knew she moved from Baltimore, but Annapolis wasn't so very far away. And they bought the row house, but that would eventually prove to be an investment, hopefully. What else was there? Didn't she love the way it felt to cuddle each other in the early mornings before the alarm clock rang? Didn't she love the way their hands slipped into each other's when they walked side by side? They discussed the remark until the wee hours of the morning that night until Michelle finally agreed to give the bookstore—and the row house—a six-month trial.

Brian bought the store lock, stock, and barrel two weeks later. The former owner was retiring and all too happy to sell the struggling business. But Brian had bigger plans and he knew the location was ideal. Luanne helped repaint the drab yellow walls in yet another shade of soft gray that Michelle selected. His mother also showed a talent for window displays. The coffee bar was added at her suggestion and proved to be a big money maker. In fact, most days, he sold more lattes than novels.

Since then, Brian couldn't have been happier going to work every day. He loved the smell of the place and the feel of the books as he stacked them on the shelves. It was a hand-to-mouth existence, especially during that first long winter. Some weeks, he dipped into his shrinking savings account to make ends meet. Other weeks, he came out ahead and had money left over to put back into the bank.

Four months after the store opened, Brian jumped the gun and declared the bookstore to be profitable, although just barely. After that, his marriage went straight downhill.

Chapter Nine

Brian arrived at work early to find five women standing in front of the store.

"Good morning, ladies," he said, unlocking the door. "What brings you out this early?"

"Anna Waters, of course," said one raven-haired woman in a tennis outfit. "This is where she's holding her book signing, isn't it?"

"Yes," Brian said. "But that isn't for another hour."

"I know," she said. "But I wanted to get here early. I wanted to be sure I got a copy of her new book. Besides, it's so pretty outside."

Not wanting to leave his customers standing on the sidewalk, Brian flipped the sign to OPEN and let the ladies in. "I haven't made the coffee yet," he said. "But that'll only take ten minutes or so. Please feel free to browse around the store."

The women filed inside, chattering excitedly amongst

themselves. All five went directly to the table Brian had set up the night before for Anna Waters. He'd draped orange crepe paper around the sides and stacked copies of the new novel on every corner. A large poster board of the beautifully illustrated cover stood on an easel behind the chair that Brian hoped would be comfortable enough for the day's event.

"Here it is," said one of the women.

"I like the cover," said another. "I wonder what part of the bay it was taken from."

"Hard to say," said the first woman. "That's part of the fun, though, isn't it?"

Brian had not yet read *Murder in Orange*, but he'd found the other two Anna Waters novels he recently read impossible to put down. They took his mind off missing Michelle.

"If I'd known that Ms. Waters's books were so popular, I would have ordered more copies," he told the women.

"I just discovered her myself," the woman in the tennis outfit said. "A friend recommended her to me. I had no idea she was a local author. Now, I'm hooked. I'm hoping she'll come as a guest speaker to my book club."

Just then, the bells on the front door jingled and two other people came into the store, this time men. A moment later the bells chimed again and four teenagers entered. Brian's store had never seen this much business this early. "Is she here yet?" a teenaged girl asked no one in particular.

"Ten o'clock."

Brian busied himself with making coffee. The bakery delivery was not scheduled for another half-hour, but he wasn't worried. The customers seemed content to browse through the racks of books. Every single person picked up a copy of *Murder in Orange.*

The bells chimed again and in walked Jenny Sullivan, wearing a bright orange sleeveless blouse and smiling from ear to ear. She was beautiful.

"Hi," Brian called from the espresso machine. "I'm glad you're here."

"Hi," she said, making her way to him. "Are you ready for this?"

"I hope so. I didn't expect such a crowd, but I'm not complaining. It's going to be a busy day. My parents will be here. And maybe my . . . wife." Brian had called Michelle and left a message on her answering machine inviting her to the book signing. She hadn't called back, but he was hopeful that she'd make the trip.

"Have you spoken with Anna?" he asked, changing the subject.

"I called her last night," Jenny said, leaning over the counter. Once again, Brian was struck by how sweet and pretty she was. "I asked her if she needed a ride. She doesn't drive. She said she wanted to hoof it."

"I would have been happy to drive her here."

"I offered, although her husband doesn't mind driving her any place she needs to go. Anna prefers to walk most of the time. She hates traffic and refers to cars as 'horseless buggies.' She has particular animosity towards super-sized SUV's."

"Fortunately, I take my bike to and from work,"

A Dreamer's Romance 63

Brian said, wondering what other quirks of personality Anna Waters would demonstrate over the course of the day. "And I drive a sedan."

"Oh, no!" Jenny gasped, noticing the long table. "The books are almost gone! I'd better get a copy now."

"I thought you already had one."

"I want one to send my father. How many did you order?"

"Apparently not nearly enough, but I have another case or two in the back."

"You'd better go get them," Jenny said, and quickly walked to the book signing table.

The bells jingled again and then again. Brian didn't notice when Anna Waters slipped into the store, and none of the other customers did either. The author was not a woman who stood out in a crowd. She wore sneakers, blue jeans and a navy blue sweatshirt emblazoned with three red crabs. She wore no make-up and her red curls had been impatiently brushed back into a tight wad of a ponytail. She walked over to the long table where Brian had recently emptied the last case of books and sat down and picked up a pen.

"Who's first?" she asked, but no one took notice.

"I guess I am," Jenny said, finally spotting her.

"As it should be," Anna quipped as the other customers rushed to form a line behind Jenny.

The rest of the morning was a blur. Brian was too busy serving coffee and muffins and ringing up sales to speak to, much less notice, Anna Waters. But he wasn't worried. Every time he glanced her way, she was in the midst of an animated conversation with one of her devoted fans. Her appearance gave the initial impression that she was just another Chesapeake Bay native out running errands on a Saturday morning. But her conversation skills were as quick-witted as her writing. Her bright green eyes and sharp tongue quickly dispelled any notion that Anna Waters was average in any way or form. At the same time, she somehow conveyed the impression that she had something in common with everyone she spoke with. Everyone she met walked away thinking of her as a new friend.

Brian stopped looking up every time the front door bells jingled so he didn't notice when his parents arrived. They mingled around the store, chatting it up with the customers and picking out armloads of books, until the crowd around the book signing table thinned.

"Isn't this a lovely place?" Luanne McKenzie said to no one in particular when she finally took her place in line. "I'm going to come back here at least once a week and buy as many books as I can carry. This is much nicer than any of those hideous bookstore chains. They're so impersonal! You'd have to be crazy to shop for books anywhere else but in this wonderful shop. It's in such a lovely part of town. And did you try the coffee? I've never tasted better. It's absolutely out of this world!" She repeated similar sentiments again and again as she waited in line for Anna Waters to sign her copy of *Murder in Orange*.

"Mrs. McKenzie, I presume," Anna said when Luanne finally made it to the head of the line.

"How'd you know?" Luanne asked, genuinely surprised.

"Just a guess."

"I see your skills as a sleuth were not exaggerated."

"Yes," Anna said dryly. "I'm quite the master of detective work, aren't I?"

Luanne shrugged. "Okay," she said. "So I'm the owner's mother. So what? What are you going to do about it? Call a cop?"

"No," Anna said, sizing her up with a sharp expression on her face. "Quite the contrary, Mrs. McKenzie, I was going to tell you that your son is a lovely chap. Bright and astute. In spite of his brief career faux pas, of course."

"Beg pardon?"

"I was referring to his vocation as an attorney."

"Well, he's still an attorney, of course. And he may take it up again."

"Possibly," Anna said. "Then again, maybe not. And your husband is Simon McKenzie?"

"Yes. How'd you know?"

"I saw him when you both came in and I recognized him from his pictures in the newspapers, but I would have known he was a lawyer even if I hadn't seen the pictures. I too am married to an attorney, although when I first met him he was an accountant and couldn't have known the way things would turn out. I've made the best of it, however, and over the years, I've learned to spot a lawyer from fifty paces. I suspect that you can too."

"Yes," Luanne said. "They seem to have a clearly identifiable nuance to them, don't they? But, then again, that could be just my impression. You see, I'm surrounded by lawyers. My older son and my daughter are attorneys too. Brian is the only one of my offspring to have escaped from living in the belly of the beast, and that was just by the skin of his teeth."

"I have two attorney sons, but my youngest just graduated from dental school."

The two women were now smiling at each other. Luanne wanted to stay longer to talk to the eccentric writer, but there were two other people behind her in line. So she thanked the author and prepared to walk away.

"Hang around," Anna ordered, before Luanne could take a step. "I sense we have more in common. A têté-à-tête may prove to be stimulating—that is, if you have some free time?"

"I do," Luanne said.

"I will humbly sign my John Hancock for these wonderful and patient citizens and then I would be delighted if you would join me for a hot cup of joe. That is, if you're charming son would be so persuaded to indulge me in this undertaking."

"Consider yourself indulged," Luanne said. She then found Brian and informed him she'd be hijacking his star attraction. By then, the day had melted into late afternoon and the line had finally slowed to a trickle. Anna signed the last of the books, rose from her seat, curtsied to the room and announced loudly that it was "time to scoot." She then spent the next two hours sitting at a corner table in deep conversation with Luanne.

The two women were a sight. Luanne McKenzie was dressed in an expensive designer outfit consisting of fashionable black slacks with a coordinating black-

and-white checked blouse. Anna, on the other hand, clearly had little interest in fashion. Yet there was something about them that seemed identical. They both had the same bright, sharp eyes and the same fast and impatient way of talking.

Jenny tried to join them, but was quickly frightened away by the tone of the conversation between the two women. Anna would hurl a biting sentence at Luanne, who would then respond with something equally stinging. Nothing said between them was befitting of middle-aged, upper-class women of their social standing, but neither would have it any other way. After they surmised they were on equal footing as conversationalists, they set about the business of getting to know the other's likes and dislikes. There was much grumbling about lawyers and even more about the "scoundrels" in the business section of the newspaper, but it was soon clear to both Anna and Luanne that they held much of the same standards about everything from politics to fish bait.

Jenny later told Brian it was like watching a verbal tennis match between opponents of similar skill. Both Anna and Luanne had a merry glint in their eyes, and it was clear to anyone who dared get close enough they were having a wonderful time.

"I told you my mother wasn't shy," Brian said.

"It's like they're identical twins from different mothers," Jenny said, shaking her head in amazement.

"This is a nightmare," Simon added. "Frank Monson's wife! I don't think Annapolis is a big enough town for two Luanne McKenzie's, especially if they've combined forces! There's no telling what mayhem awaits all of us."

Simon, Brian, and Jenny huddled near the cash register, sipping coffee while Brian rang up any customers who happened to wander in. Occasionally one of them would nervously glance toward Luanne and Anna, who were now laughing loudly together, as if they'd known each other their entire lives. It seemed as if the battle of wits between them had been fought and declared a draw. Each now considered the other to be a worthy opponent.

When it appeared as if Anna and Luanne had finally run out of conversation, Jenny offered her a ride home.

"No thanks, kiddo," she said. "Mrs. McK has already kindly extended the same invitation."

Brian waited for his parents and Anna to go before he closed up the shop while Jenny straightened up the ravaged bookshelves. It was an hour past closing time before he was able to finally flip the door sign to CLOSED and lock the front door.

"That was a screaming success," Jenny said.

"Yes," Brian said. "Thank you for introducing me to Anna. It's the biggest day my store's ever seen. Can I give you a ride home?"

"No," she said. "I have my car."

"Good, because I rode my bike and you might not find the handlebars very comfortable. Where are you parked? Let me walk you."

"I'm just around the corner," she said. Her eyes were sparkling and she was smiling. Brian could see that she was still excited about the day. They rounded the corner and he fought the urge to take her hand in his. He wasn't making a pass—it just felt like the natural thing to do. As if it was supposed to happen. Then he remembered that he was still a married man. And still missing his wife.

"Wasn't that fun?" Jenny said. "I'm so happy it went well. I was worried Anna would have a miserable time. She can be quite reclusive. And Luanne! Anna and your mom sure hit it off. What a great mother she must be! You're blessed."

"Oh, I'm blessed all right." Brian said, smiling. "But it's a mixed blessing. How about you? Any family in town?"

"No," Jenny said, a shadow falling across her face. "My mother passed away when I was a teenager. My father moved to Florida a few years ago. We talk on the phone a lot, though."

"I'm sorry," he said. "I didn't mean to bring up any unhappy times."

"It's okay," Jenny said. "I had a terrific mother. I was blessed too. I missed her during my teen years. I guess that's why I'm so drawn to Anna. She's been like a surrogate mom to me over the past few years." She stopped in front of a restored powder blue Mustang convertible. "This is me," she said, pulling out a key ring.

"Whoa," he said. "You didn't tell me you drove a car like this! What year is it? 1967?"

"You know your cars," Jenny said. "This is my baby. It was my mother's car. My father spent a full year fixing her up for me when I turned sixteen. I was the envy of the whole school. Now, I only take her out on weekends. During the week, I drive a very sensible four-door sedan. I thought Anna would enjoy riding home in the Mustang so I brought her out today. I was even going to take the roof down, but . . . alas."

"I'm surprised someone hasn't snatched you up," Brian said, walking around the car, looking it up and down. "If only for automotive reasons."

"I told you," she said. "I like my love life the way it is. Which reminds me, what happened to your wife today? I was looking forward to meeting her."

"Good question," Brian said, feeling his face turn red. "I don't know. I got so busy I didn't think to call her. I guess she got hung up with something."

"Next time, then," Jenny said with a smile as she climbed into the car.

"Next time it is."

Jenny then honked the horn, waved and drove off into the night, leaving Brian to wonder why Michelle hadn't come. After all, it had been three months.

Chapter Ten

Brian didn't take it well the night Michelle left. He spent the night calling her cell phone and pacing the floor. He finally fell into a fitful sleep on the sofa, but awoke the next morning hours before sunrise. Finally, not knowing what else to do, he rode his bicycle to downtown Annapolis. He somehow remembered that he was supposed to open the bookstore, but he knew being there would be impossible. Instead, he taped the GONE FISHING sign he made to the front door. Then he pedaled to his parents' house fifteen miles away and did exactly that. He took his father's tackle box and the family's small motorboat without saying a word to anyone. He knew they wouldn't mind.

It was still dark when he dropped anchor at his usual spot. He sat looking at the quiet shoreline and waited for the sun to rise. This was his favorite place on the water, although he never could understand why. There

71

was a quietness about this small section of shoreline that spoke to him. A peacefulness that at any other time would have left him feeling good about the world. It was a sliver of the Bay that usually left him feeling serene.

He watched the sunrise and thought about Michelle. Every ounce of his being hurt, every breath he took reminded him that she was gone. Why hadn't he seen it before? Why hadn't he realized how unhappy she was? Why hadn't she told him? He would have changed, he told himself. He would have stayed at the law firm. He would have sold the row house. He would have done anything to keep her.

The sky turned a deep, soft pink and life around the dark water began to stir, but Brian didn't notice. He was too lost in thoughts of his doomed marriage. He plotted and planned and tried to think of a way to convince Michelle to change her mind. But her last words rang in his ears and he knew, deep inside, that it was hopeless.

Michelle was right. He never listened to her. At least not the way she wanted him to hear her. He loved her blindly, and with that love came the mistaken notion that she wanted the same things he wanted. Even when she told him otherwise, he took it for granted that she was happy.

When the sun came up, he baited a fishhook and cast the line into the water. He'd shown the presence of mind to grab a few bottles of water from the refrigerator in his parents' boathouse, but otherwise, he had no provisions for his impromptu fishing trip. He spent the day fishing. Occasionally he caught a fish, but he would remove the hook from its mouth, grateful for the brief diversion, and throw it back into the water. Then he baited the hook again and returned to his gloomy thoughts.

Brian watched the sky grow dark again until he could barely see. Then he gazed at the blackness. *Cloudy tomorrow*, he thought to himself. *Maybe rain.* That was all he could think of now. His thoughts of Michelle had replayed so many times over, there was nothing left to think about. He was empty.

He must have dozed off, but he didn't know for how long. He hadn't remembered to wear his watch so he didn't know the time. Judging from the pitch black sky, sunrise was still a long time away. Sitting for so long on the hard seat made his legs stiff, but he didn't want to go back. Not yet. The physical discomfort was minor compared to the ache inside him. When he closed his eyes he saw Michelle, tossing back her perfect blond hair, or gazing at him with her beautiful jade eyes. Then he'd see her walking away from him and hear her last words.

When morning finally came, he fished again but he no longer bothered to bait his hook. He practiced casting his line, reeling it back, and casting again. Time passed. The water bottles he'd brought from his parents' house were gone and he was thirsty, but the sun was growing dark again when Brian headed back. The noise of the motor startled him with its loudness. The motion of the boat and the sound of the water lapping against the sides reminded him of her. The sight of his parents' dock reminded him of her too. They'd gone sailing twice and both times Michelle said she'd felt queasy. He could see her, gingerly stepping on board, perfectly coiffed in navy blue short shorts and a sun hat.

His parents' house was silent. His body ached as he climbed out of the boat and tied the lines. The night was quiet and Brian could tell it was going to rain. A lifetime of living by the water taught him to recognize every mood of the Bay. He still had on his sea legs and he felt wobbly as he walked across the short dock to the boathouse. Someone had put his bicycle inside.

Brian took a bottle of water from the mini-fridge and drank it. Then he wheeled his bike to the front of his parents' house. He took one last look at the dark stillness around him before he pedaled his bike back home.

He hated to go inside, but there was nowhere else to go. This was his home. It was all he had left. "I want to be fair," Michelle had said. The words rang in his ears as he went through his front door.

The living room looked the same. He remembered the suitcases that so recently sat in the hallway. He went into the kitchen. It, too, looked the same. He got a glass from the cabinet and poured himself orange juice. It tasted bitter but he drank it down. The thought of food didn't appeal to him, nor did the thought of going to his bed to sleep. There were too many memories there.

Instead, Brian took a shower. Then he put on an old T-shirt and gym shorts and plopped down on the sofa. He considered turning on the television, but instead pulled the throw blanket his mother had knitted over his legs and stared at the ceiling. It was hours before he finally drifted off to a restless sleep. He dreamed of

Michelle, watching him coolly, tossing her hair and walking away. He awoke and drank a glass of water, then went back to the sofa to stare at the ceiling some more. He dozed fitfully until morning, when he was awakened by a loud pounding.

"Movers," a voice shouted through the front door, over the word that repeated again and again inside of his head—gone, gone, gone.

Chapter Eleven

Luanne McKenzie remembered the day after Michelle left Brian every bit as clearly as he did. She remembered hanging up the phone and waiting for the shock of the news her husband had just delivered to subside. "Michelle just marched into my office and quit her job," Simon told her. "She said she enjoyed working with me but she was leaving for personal reasons. She also said she was divorcing Brian. She was quite professional about it—she looked like butter wouldn't melt in her mouth."

"What?" Luanne gasped, reeling.

"I asked her why," Simon continued. "But all she said was that she'd spoken with Brian and he understood her reasons. Did he call you, Lu? I'm worried about the boy. He isn't at the store. I checked. Furthermore, and I'm not implying that this has any connection to Michelle—it may be purely coincidental—there's another employee, Roger Honaker, who walked into my office fifteen minutes after Michelle left. He quit too. Neither one of them gave notice and both said they'd found jobs in Baltimore. Left me in a hell of a fix dividing up their workload between the rest of the staff, but that's the least of our problems."

Luanne made Simon repeat the story twice. "Are you sure?" she asked.

"Yes, dear. I was quite alert when she told me."

"But Brian never said a word . . ."

"I don't think he knew."

"How did he take it?"

"I don't know. There was no answer at his house when I called. I went by the store, but it was closed and there was a *Gone Fishing* sign on the door. Have you checked the boats?"

Luanne hung up the phone and went outside to the dock. She saw Brian's bike propped up against the side of the boathouse and saw that the small motorboat was gone. She knew where her son was, and she knew he wouldn't be back for awhile. Since boyhood, Brian fished when something was bothering him.

She felt a rush of anger as she quickly got dressed. "Michelle!" she seethed. She'd never much cared for her son's bride, but now the thought of her made Luanne clench her teeth. Brian had given her a spare set of keys to the bookstore to use in the event of an emergency and, to Luanne, this seemed like an emergency. Then she picked up the telephone.

"Simon," Luanne said when she heard the voice on the other end. "How'd you like to help an old battle-axe run a bookstore for a day or so?"

"Sounds mind-numbing," her husband said. "Meet you there in fifteen minutes."

The two spent the next few days learning the ropes of running a bookstore. It wasn't long before Brian's store was running like a well-oiled machine.

Chapter Twelve

By Monday Brian was home again, but he found it unbearable watching the movers carry out the furniture that had once belonged to both him and Michelle. He instructed them to do their dirty deed and let themselves out when they were through. Then he rode his bicycle into town. He parked it outside a restaurant near State Street. It was an expensive bike, but the notion of locking it up didn't occur to him in his blurry state of mind. He hadn't eaten in almost two days, but the omelet he ordered was without taste and the fullness in his stomach gave him no comfort.

Somehow, he'd remembered to check his answering machine before he left home. The flashing red light gave him a momentary spark of hope that Michelle had called, but the only message was from his father. "We know you're on the boat, Bri," Simon's booming voice said from inside the black box. "Michelle told me what happened. I know you must feel like hell, son, but I wanted to call you anyway. I want you to know that you're going to be all right. Just take things one day at a time for now. I know it doesn't seem like it will ever be right again, but one morning you'll wake up and you'll realize the sun's still shining after all. That's when you'll realize the world hasn't stopped turning. Believe it or not, son, one day you're going to feel like your old self again, and you'll be thankful that this thing with Michelle didn't go on for another twenty years . . . I mean to say . . . Look, Brian, things will work themselves out for the better in the long . . ." The answering machine beeped shrilly and Brian hit the DELETE button.

Even the clatter of the restaurant couldn't distract Brian's thoughts from the train wreck his life had become. After he ate, he rode his bike around downtown Annapolis. Annoying the morning rush hour with his existence gave him malicious pleasure until the heavy traffic slowed to the routine Monday morning buzz—busy, but not gridlocked. He made his way to the outskirts of Annapolis, sticking to the less-populated areas until he reached his parents' neighborhood. The thought of spending any more time on a boat made him feel queasy; instead he cruised through the streets for a time and then rode back to town. He made the trek, back and forth, two more times before he went home.

The two days of solitude were good for him. His head didn't feel any clearer, but he was able to slowly formulate a vague plan for the day—this day and this day only. He'd decided to paint the downstairs powder room. It was a thought that came to him like a call from the heavens after several hours of careful consideration. A decision he could get behind and cling to because it afforded him the thing he needed most—busywork.

He selected a deep butterscotch color, a shade Michelle would have hated. She much preferred mono-chromatic themes of black and white or shades of pale gray, but painting the bathroom in a color his wife was partial to would only make him think of her more. And the last thing Brian wanted to do was think. He wanted work. Back-breaking, mind-numbing, physical work that he could throw himself into. The downstairs pow-der room was the perfect project.

They'd kept the door shut since they'd moved in. The sink was inoperable, the toilet ran for fifteen full min-utes after it was flushed, and the ceramic tile floor needed to be replaced. The powder room was yet anoth-er reason why Michelle hated the house and why he adored it.

Brian realized as soon as he opened the door he wouldn't be ready to paint any time soon. The condi-tion of the walls needed to be addressed first, not to mention the broken tiles and the forty-year-old fixtures.

He took his car to the hardware store. Brian seldom drove. The only time he found the need to travel via any other method besides his bicycle was when he was with . . . He played the radio at a deafening level and concentrated on the growing list of materials he need-ed to purchase.

Two hours later, he was back at the row house unloading his car. He was ready to begin his task. The powder room would take five days to complete, working almost around the clock. Brian thought of nothing else but the work he was doing. He gutted the bathroom from floor to ceiling, scraping off the old, peeling, pink-flowered wallpaper and tearing out the floor. First, he patched and sanded down the walls until they were in pristine condition. Next, he replaced the old sink with a new one with a pedestal base. Then he hung a new light fixture and installed the new toilet. The fixtures were all in a warm ivory color. Next, he lay down the new ceramic tile. Last, Brian brushed on the butterscotch-colored paint.

He was surprised by how nice the new bathroom looked. The years of toiling under his mother's high standards of workmanship had finally paid off. He made one last trip to a department store to purchase towels and a wastebasket, hung an oval-shaped oak mirror over the sink and declared the work complete. The powder room now looked like something from the pages of a magazine.

Brian savored a fleeting moment of pleasure before he realized that there was no more work to do. All too soon, his reprieve was over and his thoughts began drifting back to Michelle. His misery washed over him again in a slow-moving wave. "It's over," he said aloud, but the words only left him feeling emptier.

Brian cleaned up the last of the dust and sighed. His mind started to race. Thank goodness there were more projects that needed his attention—both at home and at the bookstore. Days had gone by since he'd been to work and he knew it was time to go back. Brian knew by his answering machine that his mother and father were running his store and he was grateful.

He woke up early the next morning and called his mother to thank her. He told her he'd been taking care of a few things at home. A statement which was true but not necessary. Luanne told him to take all the time he needed. He took her up on her offer and requested one more day. Brian was more than ready to return to work but, unfortunately, his decision to first restore the powder room proved to be impractical due to the fact that Michelle had left him with almost no furniture, including a bed. What sleep he got was found in an old, musty-smelling sleeping bag in the empty living room. Brian needed one more day to refurnish his house.

He called a store and ordered a bed. It was delivered the same day and placed in the smallest bedroom. He spent the rest of the day on a shopping spree, buying pots and pans, dishes, silverware, and a few towels—all purchased with funds from a small savings account he'd forgotten to add Michelle's name to.

Chapter Thirteen

"Hi," Jenny said, walking into the bookstore the following Friday.

"Hi," Brian said, offering her a weak smile. He was in the children's section, unloading books from the shelves and placing them in tall stacks against the wall.

"You need a vacation?"

"Vacation?"

"Yes." She nodded, smiling. "You look exhausted."

Brian blinked at her, not sure of what to say. "I've been doing some projects around the house," he said. "But I'm back now."

"Great," she said. She was smiling brightly, just like always. "Did you read Anna's new book? I couldn't put it down. I think it's the best one yet. She says she sent *Murder in Blue* to her editor six months ago and it could come out as early as April, but I don't know if I can wait three more months. Anna says it's about the murder of a blues singer who was notoriously hated by the other members of the band. But then another band member is found murdered. And then their manager. Of course, Bux falls in love with the lead singer and has to save her."

"Sounds great."

"Oh, I know it will be. Apparently, the buzz from *Murder in Orange* has been positive and the publisher wants to release the next one as soon as possible. Anna says it could be in print in just a few months."

"I'm glad to hear that," Brian said, barely listening. He'd stayed up most of the night before painting the dining room a shade of warm sage, and he was feeling the effects of his on-going lack of sleep.

"What are you doing?" Jenny asked, tilting her head to one side.

"Huh?" Brian asked.

"Why are you taking down all the kiddie books?"

"Oh . . . um . . . I'm going to strip down the shelves and redo them with a light stain. Then I'm going to repaint the walls, probably in a primary color. I don't know. It gets pretty quiet in here during the day and I have some free time on my hands. I was thinking the color of the walls is too . . . I don't know."

"I agree," Jenny said. "Gray walls look too sterile. The children's section would be a great place for a wall mural. I could help you with the design if you'd like."

"Huh?"

Jenny was beginning to realize that Brian was not himself. "I'm sorry," she said. "I didn't mean to sound as if I was drumming up business. To tell you the truth,

I don't know when I'd find the time to help you plan a wall mural. Don't mind me, Brian. You're better off sticking with your original plan." She then excused herself and went to her favorite corner of the store, the mystery section. She remained there for almost an hour, quietly sifting through the paperbacks. She didn't call Brian when she finally made her selection. Instead, she left the money sitting on the counter next to the cash register and almost made it out the door before he called out to her.

"Jenny," he said from behind a shelf. It was hard to find the words to talk to her. He was so happy she was there, but he was so sad that Michelle was gone. "I would love a wall mural in here," he said, trying to keep his voice bright. "And I'd love it if you could somehow find the time to personally do the work. I don't care what it costs, but I'd appreciate it if you'd put me on your short list. Paint it any color you'd like, just as long as it's not gray."

Chapter Fourteen

Jenny Sullivan took a step back to examine her work. She cocked her head to one side, her brow furrowed in deep concentration. She paced back and forth, examining the wall at every possible angle while she chewed her lip and frowned.

Brian knew not to strike up a conversation; Jenny was entrenched too deeply in the task before her to make small talk. Instead, he asked Travis, the teenaged boy he'd recently hired, to take her a cup of coffee. Travis had been working at Brian's Books & Coffee Shop every weekend for the past two months because ever since Anna Waters' book signing appearance, business had slowly increased.

At first, a steady trickle of people had stopped by to pick up a copy of *Murder in Orange*, but, as the work on the mural progressed, the store became more popular. Some only bought coffee and watched Jenny as she worked; others purchased a stack of Anna Waters novels to take with them. Most came back again, if only to see how the mural was coming along. Weekends were the busiest. Jenny painted, Travis manned the coffee bar, and Brian ran the cash register.

It had been months since Jenny had begun working her magic with a paint brush. The work on the wall mural in the children's section took her almost four weeks to complete, working an hour or two a few nights a week and all day on Saturday, but the finished artwork was a masterpiece.

Jenny immediately dismissed the notion of painting the characters from children's books onto the walls. Instead, she opted for a quiet beach scene on a clear, sunny day. She used shades of blue and white for the perfect sky, and soft tans and corals for the sandy beach. There was a beautiful red lighthouse off in the distance and white and black gulls in the sky. There were seashells on the beach and sandcastles at the shore. True to her word, Jenny had not used one drop of gray paint. The mural had a three-dimensional-quality to it, as if you could step up and walk right onto the sand. It was breathtaking.

After the walls in the children's corner were complete, Jenny painted the bookshelves in bold blue and white stripes so that they looked like cabanas. She then painted the scaled-down, child-sized tables and chairs to resemble wooden picnic tables and beach chairs. The table was set with painted-on dishes that held painted-on food. The chairs had painted-on beach towels hanging over the backs and painted-on sand sticking to the legs. The colors she used were bright, but not blinding, and the scene was detailed without being too busy. It made the children's section a wonderful place to spend an hour or two looking at books.

After Jenny finished the mural in the children's section, Brian asked her to tackle the romance section, which was in the opposite corner of the store. He didn't ask to see her plans. He knew she'd come up with something wonderful. Brian was pleased when he saw that there would be no hearts and cupids adorning the walls. Instead, Jenny elected to stick with the same theme as in the children's walls. The beach scene continued down the wall and meandered along until it became a sandy pathway that led to a pretty gazebo in the romance section. The gazebo overlooked a wooden dock where a little brown rowboat with green oars was tied. She painted the tables and chairs to resemble white wrought iron furniture with painted-on glasses of iced tea and painted-on dainty yellow dishes which held painted-on sandwiches. She then painted the bookcases to resemble vine-covered lattice walls.

Brian was relieved that the mural in the romance section caused no undo reminders of his own disastrous love life. Due to the increase of business, he was able to pay Jenny a bonus, and then he asked her to tackle the mystery section.

"Thanks," Jenny said, taking the coffee from Travis. She flashed him one of her heart-melting smiles and he dreamily smiled back. She sipped the coffee and returned to studying the wall. She was painting a snack shack. She sketched out a dilapidated wooden hut on the wall in pencil and Brian could see as the paint went on the wall that there was something about the shack that was not quite as cheerful as the rest of the beach. The sky overhead was a few shades darker and more foreboding. Gone, too, were the plants and seashells in soft, gentle colors. Instead, behind the counter of the snack shack, Jenny drew a man. He was life-size and youthful, with sun-bleached blond hair and icy blue eyes, but there was a shiftiness to his handsome face that was unsettling. He leaned against the wall behind the counter, his cold eyes squinting into the distance and his arms folded across his muscular chest. There was something in the way he stood there that let you know he wasn't going to take your order any time soon. In fact, there was something about the little beach hut that was decidedly disturbing. Something dark and lurking.

Brian loved it.

"I decided not to have any bodies poking out from behind the counter," Jenny told him. "Or guns either. It might upset the kids, not to mention the romance readers."

"Ahh, yes," Brian said. "Those foolish dreamers."

"I'm sorry?"

"Remember?" He reminded her. "You once said romances were for dreamers."

She smiled. "No," she said. "I said romance *novels* were for dreamers."

Brian smiled back at her and, for a moment, their eyes locked. He felt an ache in his arms and in his heart. He wanted to take her in his arms and hold her.

"I have a confession to make," Jenny said, still looking at him shyly. "Don't tell anyone this, but I read romance books every now and then."

"Really?" he said.

"Especially after I've read a particularly grisly mystery. It's nice to get lost in something a little sweet every now and then."

Brian almost smiled, but caught himself in time. The last thing he wanted to talk about was being swept away by a romance story. He didn't believe in romance stories anymore, and he wasn't much of a dreamer either.

Six months had passed since Michelle had left him. He'd finally confessed to Jenny that he was separated. It was a difficult conversation to have, especially with Jenny, but he couldn't deny it any longer. Michelle wasn't coming back. Jenny was sympathetic and kind. In fact, sometimes it was all he could do to keep from telling her just how awful it was to go through a divorce. But he couldn't lay that at Jenny's feet. He'd never do that to her.

Six long, hard months had come and gone but to Brian, it seemed like far more. The days blended into each other in a slow-moving, hazy blur. He'd heard rumors, in small bits and pieces, told to him by people who maintained an air of curiosity and indignation. They'd told him Michelle had relocated to Baltimore and taken a job at a large law firm. They'd also mentioned that she had a "friend" she'd met at the firm in Annapolis. A friend named Roger Honaker, who'd left Hickman, Boris & McKenzie the same day as Michelle.

Brian pretended not to care. Instead, he focused his energy on redoing every room of the house his wife left behind. The downstairs powder room was just the beginning. Brian took each room, one at a time, and worked relentlessly until it was also a work of art. Then he would move on to the next project.

The work gave Brian something he needed almost as much as oxygen. He divided his time between working in the bookstore and restoring the row house. Every day after work, he'd labor well into the night on the house. It would be hours before he'd finally climb into bed and fall into an immediate, exhausted slumber that brought him little respite from his misery. But that was only on nights when his luck was with him. Insomnia plagued him and he rarely slept for more than a few hours at a stretch.

Brian first tackled the living room. He patched and sanded the walls, fixed the creaking floorboards, repaired the ancient windows where it was needed. Then he painted the walls a warm sage color. Next, came the dining room, where he repeated the process. Then came the guest bedroom, where he'd been sleeping. He painted a warm (and restful) shade of sea green.

It'd taken months to purchase the few pieces of furniture he'd collected. Brian bought as his finances allowed. Fortunately, the book store was showing a profit. In fact, some weeks he was even able to put a few dollars into his savings account. The furniture was designed in a simple, clean-lined style and there was not one iota of leather, chrome, glass, or the color gray.

After he bought a sofa in a deep green chenille fabric, Brian decided the finish of the wooden floors was too dark for his new color scheme, and set about stripping them down to bare wood and restaining them in a light finish. Luanne volunteered to help, but he turned her down cold. He'd come to take pleasure in the ache in his muscles and the soreness in his back.

Brian's present project was stripping down layers and layers of paint on the kitchen cabinets. He felt fairly certain there was wood underneath it all, and planned to find it some day. Once he did, he'd decide what color stain to use, if any. After that, he was going to do something about the worn green and tan squares of linoleum on the floor.

During the day, he took down books in his store and repainted the bookshelves white—the color Jenny instructed him to use. Then she'd paint blue stripes on them so that they'd resemble cabanas or creeping ivy on the shelves near the gazebo, or even a thatched straw "storage closet" near the snack shack.

Jenny and Brian rarely spoke to each other. Other than "hello" and "goodbye" and news of how remarkably good the sales were on Anna's new book, there was not much Brian wanted to say. He was bowled over whenever he saw her, and the sensation always left him feeling confused. How could he miss Michelle so much, yet long to be with Jenny at the same time? He wondered if Anna had told Jenny about his marital problems. He wasn't sure because Jenny never asked him about his private life, and he was grateful. Instead, she focused her attention on her art. But it was a comfortable silence between them. Jenny would paint while Brian ran the store. In this way, the two came to know each other well.

Chapter Fifteen

It wasn't long before customers started to notice the changes at Brian's Books & Coffee Shop. Business was improving steadily, especially since Anna Waters often dropped by on Saturday mornings. She'd sign a few books and schmooze with the customers and then watch Luanne while she read to the children.

The readings had started out as a bit of fun for Luanne McKenzie. She'd always been an animated reader who was blessed with a million and one voices and the facial expressions to go along with them. Brian fondly remembered the bedtime stories from his childhood, but even he'd forgotten how well his mother took to the task. She'd sit in the big rocking chair (which was painted to look like an Adirondack chair) in the children's section and read to whichever children were there. When the story called for an evil stepmother, she'd become cold and hissing. When the character was a sweet child, her voice would raise to cherubic decibels. Witches cackled, babies cooed, and fairy godmothers waved magic wands. Ducks quacked, cows mooed, and horses whinnied without any question as to their identity. It wasn't long before Luanne took to showing up at the bookstore dressed in full costume and carrying a tote bag full of hand-puppets.

The children were captivated by the stories and they never wanted to let her put down the books. Brian was soon deluged with requests asking when "Miss Lu" would arrive. Children would beg for their favorite books to be read and Luanne was only too happy to accommodate them. A chalkboard resting on an easel soon appeared by the entrance, and provided the book title and time of Luanne's next reading. Soon, her spontaneous appearances became scheduled events that were repeated twice on Friday, three times on Saturday, and once every Tuesday and Wednesday afternoon.

Today, she was dressed as a witch, complete with cape, pointed hat and long green finger nails. ". . . and then what happened?" she screeched, her face a mask of furious indignation.

"AND THEY ALL LIVED HAPPILY EVER AFTER!" shouted back the gaggle of children, some of whom were rolling on the floor in excitement.

"Yes," Luanne croaked woefully. "Unfortunately, they did do just that." She sighed in disgust. "I do hate all these happy endings, don't you?"

"Yes!" screamed back the children, laughing and flopping around on the big beach towel floor pillows Luanne had made.

"As a matter of fact, all these glad tidings have left

me feeling a bit weak." Luanne's expression was one of wicked frailty. "I think I almost smiled a moment ago, and you know how I detest smiling. The only thing that could possibly save this hideous day would be if I were to find some children wandering around the woods near my candy house. I would so enjoy inviting them in for a bite. Are there any toddlers here who would like to be . . . I mean . . . have lunch?"

"No!" shouted the children, stomping their little feet and shaking their little fists.

"No?" Luanne asked. "Very well then. Next time."

They groaned when she left the big rocking chair, but they knew from previous experience that Miss Lu was done with her reading until next time. Soon, she'd slip out of her costume and become just another ordinary adult, except, of course, for the green nail polish.

She stood up and swept the long, black cape around her dramatically before she glided across the room and disappeared behind the door marked EMPLOYEES ONLY. Sure enough, when she reappeared again, she was dressed in tan slacks and a thick red sweater. The children eyed her guardedly but didn't question her new appearance. They preferred to pretend that Miss Lu was really a witch, or a queen, or a talking unicorn, and not the grandmotherly woman she appeared to be. But that never stopped them from giving her hugs whenever they saw her.

"Nice job," Anna Waters said, handing her a cup of coffee. "You had me shaking in my topsiders today. I think I liked you better when you were Curious George. I considered notifying the authorities that there was a hag on the loose, but Brian reminded me that the books you read were selected from the fiction shelves, not the memoirs."

"Brian spoke to you?" Luanne asked, surprised.

"No," Anna said. "I just made that part up. He did say hello when I came in but then he got that panicked look in his eye again. As if I would dare ask him how he was doing. How is he doing, by the way?"

"The same," Luanne sighed. "He has bags under his eyes and I don't think he's eating well. He's lost weight. I think Christmas was difficult for him. When I ask him if he sleeps, he says he does, but I don't know if I believe him. I don't know when he has time. You should see his house. It's never looked so good. Not that he'd invite me to stop by. I sneak up on him every now and then, though. I drop by with a casserole or crab cakes. The only thing we talk about are his home improvement projects. I've offered to help him, but he won't hear of it. Currently, he's completely gutted the kitchen. Torn off every last cabinet door. He says he's stripping them down."

"By himself?"

"Yes, and that's my specialty. He says he wants to do it by himself. The McKenzies have always been handy around the house, of course, but Brian is tackling this project during the evenings after he's already spent twelve hours in this store. I'm worried about him. I told him I'd be more than happy to take on the restoration of his kitchen or, at least, run the store for him. But he's as stubborn as a billy goat—just like his father. Now look at him. He's exhausted and as thin as a rail."

"Leave him alone, Lu," Anna said.

"But it's been months! I thought he'd be coming around by now."

"Let him work it out in his own way."

"You're probably right," Luanne said, her voice worried. "You never had the pleasure of meeting my daughter-in-law, Michelle, did you?"

"No," Anna said. "But I'm sure Brian saw something in her that you missed."

Luanne shook her head. She had little patience when it came to her son's soon-to-be ex-wife. "Oh, she's quite attractive," she said, sticking her jaw out stubbornly. "But pretty is as pretty does, you know."

"Brian isn't shallow, Lu. He saw more to her than her good looks."

"Perhaps, but I can't imagine what that was."

"Has he heard from her?"

"No," Luanne said. "Not since he received the separation agreement. It seems to be going very slowly. Not that he's in a hurry."

"These things take time, but my guess is that Michelle will want to finalize the divorce sooner or later."

"Hmpf," Luanne said. "You're right. Michelle probably can't wait to be rid of Brian. That's what's so mystifying about the whole situation, Anna. Brian loved her. He worshipped the ground that horrible woman slithered on and . . ."

"Lu!"

"I'm sorry, but it's true. Michelle was a self-absorbed mannequin and Brian's better off without her."

"Luanne," Anna said, a knowing look in her eye.

"You know better than to talk that way. Trust me, I've been there. I didn't much care for my oldest son's wife at first either. She straightened up after the baby was born, though. Now that we have a common bond, we're like two peas in a pod. Fortunately, I had the good sense to keep my opinions to myself."

"I know," Luanne said. "And I did just that, or at least I tried to. I kept my opinions to myself right up until she walked out on him and left him . . . left him . . ."

"Left him what?"

"Heartbroken," Luanne whispered. She was watching Brian from across the room. He was behind the register, ringing up a customer. He was as well mannered and pleasant as always, but he wasn't the same son she used to know. Since Michelle left, he'd worn a shell-shocked, dazed expression most of the time and rarely smiled, except when he was talking to Jenny. Most of the time there was a sadness about Brian. "I don't know what he saw in her," Luanne said for the millionth time.

"I know," Anna said. "And you never will. But, right now, leave the boy alone. Time heals all wounds and wounds all heels, you know."

Luanne nodded. "I only complain to you, my dear. Simon has far less patience for my rantings than even you, if you can believe that. I don't dare say a word about Michelle to him. It might keep him from telling me the latest gossip he's heard."

"Oh? Is there any gossip?"

"Just what I've already told you. Michelle and that Roger Honaker fellow are working together at a new law firm in Baltimore. But they're not knocking them dead like they thought they would. Simon never admitted this at the time, but it's now coming out that Michelle's work tended to be a bit sloppy. He always chalked it up to her youth or that she might have been testing the waters of her family ties, but apparently things haven't improved at the Baltimore firm. Simon knows several people who know people. They tell him that the pretty lawyer out of Annapolis is close to getting herself canned. Also, there are rumors that she takes exceedingly long lunch hours with another coworker."

"Mr. Honaker, I presume?"

"Coincidentally, yes. And his work habits are not much better than hers." Luanne's cheeks turned pink as they always did when she spoke of Michelle.

"I'll ask my husband if he's heard anything," Anna said. "But in the meantime, don't get your knickers in a knot, lady. Brian is made of stronger stock. He'll survive this ordeal and be a better man for it in the end. Meanwhile, you need not put up your boxing dukes every time Michelle's name is mentioned."

"He's my son, Anna."

"I hear you, sister. I have two sons of my own. But he's a grown man and, from everything I've seen, taking care of himself. Sure, it hasn't been easy. But he's getting through it in the only way he knows how—by keeping busy. Where'd he get that from? Therefore, for the purposes of public safety, I'm going to gently change the subject to an equally intriguing topic—me. My latest book comes out in two months."

"Finally, *Murder in Blue*?"

"Yes, and my editor just finished reviewing *Murder in Green.* That will be released within the year. Meanwhile, I've started writing *Murder in Red*, and I have an idea for the plot of the one after that. I'm going to call it *Murder in Brown.*"

"My heavens. You and Brian must take the same vitamins. How on earth did you finish so many books so soon?"

"My editor already had my draft of *Murder in Blue* and I was almost finished with *Murder in Green* when *Murder in Orange* was released. As you know, sales have been positive, so my editor asked me to get going on the next one. The truth of the matter is that the plots for the books have been in my head for a long time. Most of my stories are well-formed by the time I actually get down to the business of putting them on paper. I work for four hours every morning. Of course, it doesn't hurt that my editor calls me every day to check on my progress. It's coming along, paragraph by paragraph, page by page. I'll keep going until my well runs dry, although I don't know how many more Bux McGee books I have left in me."

"Your well will never run dry," Luanne noted. "Will you do another signing for Brian?"

"Absolutely," Anna said. "Brian's Books & Coffee Shop is the only place I'd consider holding a book signing. My editor wants me to do a tour, but I told him I was too busy writing. He's happy with that as long as I can get the area newspapers to review my next book."

"Did you?" Luanne asked.

"Yes," Anna said. "They've both agreed to write a

blurb about my books, and I think the *Baltimore Post* might even be persuaded to visit the book signing. My editor thinks that would give my sales a good kick in the pants."

"Your sales are already pretty hot around here."

"Of course they are. The novels are set in Annapolis."

"I don't know," Luanne said. "It looks like your books are becoming a hit everywhere. Now that we're done talking about you, my dear, can I get back to bad-mouthing Michelle?"

"You have five minutes," Anna said, looking at her watch. "After that, we'll move on to the next topic. Brian is coming back to life, Lu. It's been hard, but he's coming back."

Chapter Sixteen

Three women were waiting patiently in line when Brian pedaled up to his store. It was the usual Anna Waters devotees, who'd become his regular customers.

"Good morning, Rosie," he said, greeting them as he parked and locked his bicycle. "Janet, Sherry, you ladies are out and about early this morning. Come on in. I'll make coffee while you browse."

"Oh, no, Brian," one of them said. "You don't open for another fifteen minutes. We're just early birds out enjoying this unseasonably warm weather. We'll wait until you open."

"For you three," he said, "my store never closes. But Anna won't be here for almost another hour."

"We know. We wanted to have a latte and look around a bit. This is our favorite bookstore."

"And you're my favorite customers." Brian smiled. He loved chatting it up with the regulars. He unlocked the front door and the women followed behind him, then he turned on the lights and flipped the CLOSED sign to OPEN. Travis was not scheduled to arrive for another few minutes, so he began making the coffee while the women hunted down the table he'd prepared for Anna the night before. Copies of her latest book were stacked neatly in piles on top and still more were stacked on a nearby fold-out card table. Luanne had donated a lace tablecloth dyed to a deep shade of blue for the event, and would be bringing a bundle of balloons—blue, of course—in a matter of minutes.

"This cover is better than the last one," one of the women said, picking up a book.

"I love it! Anna didn't mention that the artwork was going to be so elaborate."

"It's no more elaborate than the last one. But that's our Jenny."

"It's breathtaking."

Brian stopped in his tracks. Had Jenny done the artwork for the cover of *Murder in Blue*? He felt a thrill run through him. He finished making the coffee and went to the book signing table. He hadn't seen the cover clearly the night before when he stacked the books onto the table. Brian picked up a book and examined the paper cover closely.

The customers were right—it was breathtaking. It was all in a deep shade of blue, the color of the sky right before sunset. There was a line of trees along a river bank and an empty rowboat in the water. It was a peaceful scene, but one that was draped in intrigue. The deep color, the empty boat, the quiet river—all worked together to deliver a mood that was somehow sinister and gripping. Brian suddenly recognized Jenny's eye for detail and her unmistakable brushstrokes.

There was something familiar about the picture. It took Brian only a moment to realize the scene was a landscape of his favorite spot of the Bay. The same spot where he'd taken his parents' motorboat that fateful day after Michelle left him. The same favorite spot he hadn't been to since. The art was brilliant. Brian smiled and opened the book. "Cover art by Jennifer Sullivan," it read, and a feeling of pride washed over him.

Just then, the bells on the front door jingled their unmistakable song and Anna Waters, Luanne, and Jenny walked in. "Got any coffee?" Anna asked, charging ahead in her usual bustle.

"Sure," Brian told them. "It'll be ready in a few minutes." He noticed their faces were flushed from the warm morning sun, and they looked as if they'd been having a wonderful time on the ride over.

"Jenny took the top down," Luanne told him, patting her hair. "It was a bit windy but, oh my, it felt wonderful. It's warm for April, isn't it? Does anyone have any hairspray?"

"Your hair is going to break off in pieces and fall to the floor if you don't leave it alone," Anna accused. "This is the first time I've seen you when your head doesn't look like a football helmet. Leave it alone and let it all hang out. You'll look just like Cindy Crawford."

"I get that a lot," Luanne said, smoothing down her hair. "But I don't take beauty tips from someone with your split ends."

"Well, how about a baseball cap? Or maybe that cowboy hat Simon brought you back from his trip to Houston?"

"That would hardly do, now would it?"

"Luanne McKenzie, you're a vain, conceited woman, and I'm here to tell you that no one cares one iota about your hair."

"They most certainly do!" Luanne said. "People care deeply about my hair. None of them have hair as unruly as yours, of course, but they still look to me for guidance. I wouldn't dream of letting them down. You know I don't take my responsibilities lightly." The two women snipped at each other, back and forth, while Brian made the coffee. "Good morning," Jenny said, giving him an amused smile.

"Hi," he said. "Coffee will be ready any minute." He suddenly found it difficult to look her in the eye. Why was she always so incredibly pretty? Why was she always so sweet? She wore blue jeans and a cotton button-down blouse in the same blue as the cover of Anna's book. Her hair was tousled from their morning drive, and it fell softly around her face. Her eyes were bright and she was smiling. Brian felt a tug in his chest.

"You never told me you did the cover art for Anna's books," he said.

"Oh," she said, shrugging. "I thought you knew."

"It's good. No, I take that back. It's brilliant."

"Thanks," she said, squirming under the compliment.

"It's people like you that give old crows a bad name," Anna was telling Luanne.

"Hag!" Luanne shot back.

"Battle-axe!"

"Witch!"

"Are you ready for today?" Jenny asked Brian, changing the subject.

"You don't take compliments well, do you?" Brian asked, his voice dropping. He felt suddenly warm standing next to her and had to fight the urge to take her hand. The feeling baffled him. Wasn't this his old friend? Jenny, loyal customer and painter of wall murals? Why was he suddenly tongue-tied? "You're a gifted artist," he managed to say. "And I'm sorry it took me so long to tell you."

Jenny blushed a deeper shade of red. "Thanks," she said again.

"Are you staying for the signing?"

"I wouldn't miss it for the world," she said. "Although I hope these two cool it before the authorities have to be notified. Here we go again."

". . . and your roots could use a touch up," Anna was saying to Luanne with a happy glint in her eye.

"My roots are impeccable," Luanne shot back. "And I would think that a person with fingernails such as yours . . . Have you been digging a trench with a plastic spoon, my dear? You really should consider finding a good manicurist."

Brian shrugged. "They're just getting warmed up," he said, pouring Jenny a cup of coffee. She sipped it contentedly as they watched Anna and Luanne bicker.

"It's nice to see Anna's having a good time," Jenny noted. "She's been so busy with her writing lately."

"What difference does it make if your hair is presentable?" Luanne snarled. "You're as old as dirt and . . ."

"My dear woman, I know for a fact that you went to high school with Methuselah."

"How dare you!"

"Good comeback, cookie. I'm speechless over your sparkling sentence structure."

All too soon, however, their fun ended with the ring of the bells on the front door. In marched Travis, followed by a group of three women and two men. Anna and Luanne declared a reluctant truce, claimed their coffee cups, and found their respective places—Anna at the long table and Luanne in the rocking chair of the children's section. The predicted busy day had begun.

The next several hours were a whirlwind of activity. Brian helped Travis serve coffee while he watched the cash register. He answered the customer's questions and directed the children to the big rocking chair, where Luanne read to them, one book after another, while their parents waited in the long line for Anna to sign their copy of *Murder in Blue*. Brian was barely able to look up for the next few hours, but when he did his eyes seemed to always seek out Jenny. She'd foregone her painting for the day. She was down to the last minute touches in the mystery section, but a crowded store was not conducive to her work. Instead, she helped Travis at the coffee bar and milled around Anna's table, bringing her more coffee and making certain the line moved smoothly.

"You don't work here," Brian said. "And you're not an indentured servant."

"I know," Jenny said. "I promised Anna I would hang out and wait for her while she signed her books. Am I driving you crazy?"

Yes, Brian wanted to tell her. "No," he said. "But you don't have to work. Travis and I can hold back this ugly mob."

She smiled again. "It's no trouble to pour coffee while I wait. Besides, the reporter from the newspaper should be here any minute. This could be a huge break for Anna's career."

The bells clanged again as they spoke. The jingle of the door bells was certainly not a unique event, especially during an Anna Waters book signing, but Brian knew even before he'd turned around the reporter had arrived. He watched two men make their way to the checkout counter. One man was holding an enormous, expensive-looking camera, while the other man walked around the store. It was this man that disturbed Brian the most.

"Hello," said the man when he spotted Brian. "I'm Chip Matthews. I'm with the *Baltimore Post*."

Chip? Brian thought to himself. *What kind of name is Chip?* "Hi," he said and shook his hand. "I'm Brian McKenzie. Thanks for coming out."

"Nice place," Chip said. "Especially the walls. Great artwork. I've never seen anything like it." Chip Matthews was a young man—much younger than Brian thought a reporter should be—with curly black hair and lively brown eyes. He was tall and well-built and he moved with a confidence that belied his youth. He was handsome, in a smooth, fluid way that suggested he'd seen many adventures in his young life.

"Jenny painted the murals," Rosie, the regular customer, offered, overhearing their conversation.

"Jenny?"

"Jenny Sullivan," Brian said, hesitantly introducing the woman standing next to him behind the counter. "Jenny, this is the reporter from Baltimore."

"Hello," she said, extending her hand.

Brian felt his stomach drop because he knew, even before it happened, what Chip Matthews's reaction would be.

"Gorgeous," Chip said, smiling at her as he took her hand. "The murals, I mean. They're absolutely gorgeous. You'll have to tell me all about yourself, Ms. Sullivan. I'd like to include you in the article I'm writing."

"Thank you," she said. "But this is Anna's article."

"Of course it is. But I plan to mention the bookstore and your lovely art as well."

"Yes," she said. "By all means. Isn't this a terrific place?"

"Yes," Chip said. "It is. Do you know Ms. Waters personally?"

"Yes, and I'm a customer . . . and a friend of Brian's. He's the owner of the store." Chip barely acknowledged Brian. He only had eyes for Jenny.

"Tell me about your murals."

"There isn't much to tell. Brian asked me to paint a mural for the children's section and . . . Well, one thing led to another and before you know it, we ended up painting every wall. I was lucky. There was good light, and Brian was very accommodating with my schedule."

"It's incredible."

"She also painted the cover artwork for *Murder in Blue*," Rosie interrupted again. "She does all Anna's covers." Brian wanted to show Rosie the door, good customer or not, along with Chip Matthews. At the same time, he couldn't help but feel a swell of pride for Jenny. But still, he didn't like the way Chip was looking at her, like a prospector who'd found gold in an outhouse.

The reporter's eyebrows shot up. "You did the cover illustrations too?" he asked.

"Yes," she said modestly.

"Anna Waters is over there at the table," Brian said. "I'll show you the way if you'd like."

"Thanks," Chip said, but he was watching Jenny. "Would you mind saving a moment or two for me before I leave, Ms. Sullivan? I'd like a tour of the store and an interview, if you don't mind."

"Call me Jenny," she said. "And I'll be here."

Brian escorted the annoying reporter to Anna Waters's table. He didn't like the sparks that were flying between Chip and Jenny, but there wasn't much he could do about it. Hadn't she been there, right in front of his face, for months now? Why hadn't he noticed her sooner? Brian knew the answer to that one was simple. Because I'm married—he almost said the sentence aloud.

He hadn't seen Michelle in close to nine months and it'd taken him every minute of that time to recover from their break-up. It was just over the past month that he was able to feel anything but the hard, dull ache that had lived in his chest for so long. Ironically, his return to the living happened just like his father had said it would. Brian woke up one morning and saw the sun peeking in through the new wooden blinds of his makeshift bedroom. He'd slept a full seven hours the night before. He even drank his coffee on the patio. It was the first time since she'd left that he noticed it was going to be a beautiful day.

Brian watched while Chip interviewed Anna in between her signing her book for the customers. The reporter seemed every bit as attentive to the author as he'd been to the artist, but Brian still kept a close eye on him.

Later, Chip found Jenny and took her to a table in the romance section, where they talked quietly. It seemed to Brian as if the interview with Jenny lasted much longer than it should, certainly longer than the inter-view with Anna Waters. All the while, the photographer went around the store, snapping pictures of everyone and making a general nuisance of himself.

"There you are," Jenny said, taking Brian by the hand. "Mr. Matthews would like a tour of the store. He's waiting by the gazebo."

"Great," Brian said, feeling certain the first stop should be the exit.

"Hello again," Chip Matthews said, leaning against a bookcase. "I know you're busy, Mr. McKenzie. It's perfectly fine with me if Ms. Sullivan shows me around."

"No problem," Brian said. "Allow me. Everything worth seeing is on the walls. Otherwise, we're a small, humble bookstore."

"You're being modest. How long have you been here?"

"Two years."

"Really?" Chip asked. "I thought you'd been here longer. Did you have another store before opening this one in Annapolis?"

"No, Brian said, feeling suddenly embarrassed. "I was an attorney in town."

"No kidding?" Chip said. "By any chance are you connected to Hickman, Boris & McKenzie?"

"Yes. My father is Simon McKenzie. He's here . . . somewhere. He's an attorney too. I worked with my father for a few years before I opened the store."

"That was quite a gamble, wasn't it?"

"I never saw it that way."

Chip Matthews nodded; for the first time he seemed interested in speaking with Brian. "It's a gamble that paid off well, isn't it?"

"I don't know about that. I'm happy with it," Brian said, not mentioning the toll the store had taken on his marriage. Instead he led the reporter around the store, section by section, so that he could see Jenny's artwork close up. If she wouldn't toot her own horn, Brian suddenly decided, he'd do it for her. "Jenny did this snack shack in the mystery section. As you can see, it resembles an Anna Waters book cover."

"Excellent job, Jenny."

"In the center of the store are the reference books.

Jenny painted the shelves to look like little fisherman's huts. Notice the crab traps? They're perfect in every detail. We also have a section for biographies. Jenny painted that shelf to resemble a bait shop. The bookshelves in the business section resemble a sandcastle."

"Brian built the tower," Jenny added. "He's an excellent carpenter."

"The paint she used has sand mixed in and gives the surface a gritty texture," Brian said. "Feel it."

Chip ran his hand over the side of the bookcase. "Wow," he said. "I've never seen anything like this. You have an incredible imagination."

"Imagination and talent," Brian added. "She's gifted."

"Oh, stop," Jenny said, and then gestured for them to keep going. But her pink cheeks told Brian that she was not accustomed to the steady stream of compliments.

Chip Matthews smiled. "This has been great. And I thought I'd be covering a boring book signing. Instead, I met an author who puts A. Conan Doyle to shame, found a great place to buy books, and met a talented artist. Thank you for the tour, Brian. Jenny. I can see that my work here is done. That is, if I can find my photographer . . ."

Jenny smiled. "He was talking to Anna."

"I'd better save him." Chip shook Jenny's hand one last time. Brian noticed the way he gazed into her eyes and held her hand too long. "I'll see you soon," he said softly.

"Okay."

Chip finally walked away to look for the photographer.

"Wow," Travis said when the two finally left. "I thought they'd never get out of here."

"Me too," Brian said.

"I don't know," Jenny said. "I thought they were nice."

Brian noticed the dreamy look in her eye and cringed.

Chapter Seventeen

"Read it again," Luanne said to Simon.

"I've read it three times already," he griped. "How about you read it this time, my rose. You're the one blessed with the lilting voice."

"Very well, sir, pass it here." Luanne took the newspaper eagerly and began to read the article about Anna's book signing. " 'A critique of the latest Anna Waters thriller, *Murder in Orange*, would not be complete without first telling you a little about Ms. Waters herself. She's a delightful woman with curly red hair, bright green eyes and a gentle repose . . .' "

" 'Gentle repose,' my foot," Simon said. "That woman teases wolves for sport!"

"Shh," Luanne said. " '. . . gentle repose, but don't let Ms. Waters's appearance fool you. Beneath the grandmotherly façade lies a brilliant criminal mind. Fortunately for Annapolis, Ms. Waters has focused her considerable talents on writing mystery novels. Her first book, *A Chesapeake Murder*, was written nine years ago and was quickly followed by *The False Alarm Murders* and *Murder Bay*. All three works were received warmly by the critics, but sales didn't take off. Then came *Green Water Death* and *One Man's Murder*, with sales that were steady but far from spectacular.

" 'As most of you know by now, however, all that has changed. Ever since writing *Murder in Orange*, Anna Waters has proven herself to be one of the most popular mystery writers of our time. The demand for anything written by Anna Waters has gone through the roof. *Murder in Pink*, the first book of the series, introduced us to Detective Bux McGee, a down-on-his-luck cop who relentlessly pursues suspected murderers with almost the same fervor that he pursues people who violate crabbing regulations. Yes, it's true. Detective McGee loves the Chesapeake Bay, and nothing annoys him more than crabbers who refuse to throw back the little ones. And trust me on this one; you don't want to annoy Detective McGee.

" 'Next came *Murder in White*, where Bux solves the mystery of the murdered bride. Then came *Murder in Orange*, where Bux is called upon to unravel the mysterious death of a retired citrus farmer who has come to reside by the waters of our own Chesapeake Bay. The latest novel, *Murder in Blue*, is once again set in beautiful Annapolis, Maryland, where . . .' "

"Skip over the critique," Simon ordered. "We've all read Anna's books and we know the plots. Get to the part about Brian's store."

"Oh, all right," Luanne said. "But if Anna were here, she'd have your hide. 'On Saturday, Anna Waters made a rare appearance at Brian's Books & Coffee Shop, located in downtown Annapolis. Apparently, Ms. Waters only does book signings at this location. It soon became obvious why. Although Brian's Books & Coffee Shop is barely in its second year, it has quickly become an Annapolis treasure.' "

"I like that part," Simon interrupted. "Don't you, son? 'Annapolis treasure.' Has a nice ring to it, doesn't it?"

"Shh!" Luanne said. "May I continue?"

"Of course."

" 'Tucked away on a quiet corner not far from the harbor, the store is a delight to the eye and to the soul— especially if you happen to be an avid reader. Brian McKenzie, recovering attorney and Annapolis native, told me he's always wanted to open a bookstore. And what a bookstore it is! The walls are painted in scenes that depict life along the Chesapeake Bay, but they're more than that. They're fabulous murals, the likes of which are found only in fine museums.

" 'The works were created by artist Jennifer Sullivan, another Annapolis local, who also coincidentally does the cover artwork for all the Bux McGee books, including *Murder in Orange* and *Murder in Blue*. Ms. Sullivan was present at the book signing, and I had the pleasure of meeting this charming and beautiful woman. She told me the inspiration for her artwork comes from real places along the Bay. In fact, it is a popular game among Annapolis natives to guess exactly where the scenes depicted come from.

" 'In the children's books section, a delightful woman reads to a group of children. I was not able to find out the identity of this woman—' "

"Only because he never asked," Simon said bitterly.

" '. . . but she has a wonderful voice and an animated reading style that held the attention of many a fidgety youngster . . .' Blah, blah, blah. You know the rest. 'In summary, dear readers, *Murder in Orange*, by Anna Waters, is the best mystery novel I've *ever* read (the ending will make your head explode). Furthermore, do yourself a favor and buy your copy at Brian's Books & Coffee Shop. This place is worth the trip. And, last but not least, to the lovely Ms. Sullivan, are you busy Saturday night?' "

"Are reporters allowed to do that?" Brian asked, annoyed. "Ask a woman on a date in print? Shouldn't he be reprimanded for doing something like that?"

"Oh, I don't know," Luanne said. "I don't think Jenny minds. She seemed rather charmed by Mr. Matthews."

Brian said nothing, but his jaw clenched. The idea of Jenny charmed by the dangerously handsome and confident Chip Matthews was disturbing, to say the least.

"They're going out to dinner," Luanne added.

"No!" Brian said.

"Yes. He called her and asked her if she had an answer to the question he posed in his article. They're going to The Chart House and then to that new blues club downtown. Anna said Jenny was walking on air when she told her."

"She can't!"

"Why not?" Simon asked.

"It's just that . . ." Brian stammered. "It's just that I'm not so sure about this Chip Matthews guy. He strikes me as a bit of ladies' man. Besides, Jenny's told me on more than one occasion that she likes her life just the way it is. She's a private person and she isn't interested in dating anyone."

Luanne was shaking her head. "Are you nuts? In case you haven't noticed, Jenny is a beautiful woman, and she's only human, Brian, not to mention fully capable of deciding who she wants to see. Private person or not, Jenny needs a little romance just as much as anyone."

"Romances are for dreamers," Brian muttered to himself.

"What was that, son?" Simon asked.

"Nothing," he said. "And it's perfectly all right with me if Jenny has a . . . fling, as long as he isn't some creep."

"Creep?" Simon said, realization dawning on his face. "Oh, I get it. It took you long enough to notice, son. You've finally seen the light and realized what a pretty and talented gal Jenny is! Come now, Brian, you can't expect her to wait around while you nurse your wounds and . . ."

"Simon!" Luanne said sharply.

"Hold on a minute!" Brian said. "First of all, I never expected anyone to wait while I nursed my wounds. My wounds aren't anyone's business! Second, of course I noticed Jenny was beautiful and talented. I'm not blind."

"I said pretty. You said beautiful. Why don't you tell Jenny that?"

"Because, Pop," Brian said angrily. "I'm not a player in the game, remember? I've been benched."

"I know what you're going to say, son, and as far as I'm concerned that's a moot point."

"It may be a moot point to you, but it isn't to me. I'm still married to Michelle, and although I admit I wasn't the best of husbands, I was faithful to her. I'm still faithful."

Simon began to say something, but caught himself in time.

"That's enough," Luanne said, grabbing hold of her husband's wrist and squeezing it tightly. "Simon, leave the boy alone. His love life is none of your business!"

"I know," Simon said gruffly. "I'm sorry, son. It's just that I like Jenny. She's the sweetest girl I've ever met, with the exception of your mother, of course. You're a fool if you let her get away. And not just any fool, you're a damned fool!"

"I'm married!" Brian said hotly. "What sane woman would want to get involved with the mess I've made of my life? Besides, I thought you liked Michelle."

"I never said that," Simon said.

"You never said you didn't."

"I keep my opinions to myself, unlike your mother and Huckleberry." The sleeping dog lying at their feet stirred at the sound of his name.

"Couldn't you have told me?"

"I wanted to tell you, but . . ."

"I wouldn't have listened?"

"Yes," Simon admitted.

"Tell me now," Brian said.

"What good would that do?"

"It might give me some perspective. I still don't know how I messed up."

Simon sighed and gave Luanne a guarded glance. "Do you really want to know?"

"Yes."

"Very well. I'll tell you, but you may not like what I have to say."

"Say it anyway."

Simon sighed and began. "I always suspected Michelle was more interested in marrying the McKenzie name than in marrying you. I'm sorry. It's a horrible thing to accuse someone of, especially if you have no evidence to support the claim. Nonetheless, it was a feeling I could never quite shake. Even after the wedding." Brian frowned, but he couldn't deny that he'd shared the same thoughts. "I also thought that she was too fancy for us."

"Too fancy?" Brian asked.

"Yes, what with the expensive clothes and the way she had of looking down her nose at the secretaries in the office."

"I never noticed that."

"The administrative staff certainly did! I can't tell you how many complaints I received. And her work quality was . . . not always up to par."

"You never told me that either."

"I didn't dare say a word against Michelle," Simon said. "Even in the office. I let Hickman deal with her when there was a problem. You were in love with her."

"Yes, I was," Brian admitted. "But it's over."

"Is it?" Simon asked.

"Yes."

"Because she left you?" asked Luanne, daring to speak. "Or because you don't love her anymore?"

"I don't know," Brian said. "I would have stayed with Michelle forever, but she didn't want me. Even now, I don't know how much of my feelings are wounded pride and how much are a sense of loss."

"A little of both," Simon said.

"Yes," Brian said. "But, either way, she's gone. I'm ready to move ahead with my life. In three months, the divorce will be final. Maybe then I'll have more perspective. Meanwhile, I'm staying out of the dating game."

Chapter Eighteen

Brian walked into the front door of his row house and threw down his keys on the coffee table. He was still annoyed with his father, and he didn't know why. He replayed their conversation in his head and, no matter what, he couldn't make himself sound reasonable. Why was he so angry? What was it his father had said that was so outrageous?

The McKenzies were a brood that didn't mince words, and if Simon McKenzie called you a damned fool, you could rest assured you were a damned fool— no ifs, ands, or buts about it.

Brian walked into the kitchen, looking around as he went. The cabinets had turned out even better than he'd hoped they would. The dark golden yellow he'd painted the walls served to make the freshly restored cabinets look even better. Brian went through the kitchen and out the back door onto the rebuilt porch and then down to the yard. The stone patio he'd laid worked together with the brick grill and the new landscaping to make the backyard a pleasant place to be. The work needed to complete the job was too much for him to do alone, however, and ultimately, Luanne, Simon, and Travis had helped with the heavy labor.

After walking around the yard for a while, Brian went back inside, past the powder room that started it all and into the living room. Then he went up the stairs and into the guest room where he'd set up his sleeping quarters. Almost every room was done. Almost every room was now scrubbed clean, repainted, refurnished, and restored in every detail. The furnace had been serviced; central air conditioning had been installed; the floors had been stripped, sanded and restained. All of which was financed by the recent flush of business from the bookstore. Brian's bank account was even slowly coming back to life. There was only one thing left that needed his attention—the master bedroom he'd once shared with Michelle.

Brian pushed open the bedroom door that had been shut since she'd left. He was surprised by the relative neatness he saw. Empty, but neat. His mother must have been there, he surmised, but he knew she wouldn't have done that. The black lacquered bedroom furniture was long gone, and now resided in a Baltimore condominium near the inner harbor. He walked around the room, peeking into the closet and looking out the windows. It was a much bigger space than the one he now occupied and it overlooked the back of the house, not the noisy street out front. Brian poked around the room some more and felt . . . nothing.

Brian felt nothing as he walked around the room, except for maybe the notion that it would look good painted a deep shade of camel. Maybe he could still get the plum and brown striped chenille bedspread he'd seen at the department store. Maybe he'd put the bed against the back wall.

She's gone.

The realization occurred to him almost as an after-thought. Like a mental reminder he'd given himself to pick up some milk at the grocery store. Only this time, the phrase didn't fill his heart with sorrow. This time, Brian saw it as a sad event for both him and Michelle, but one that was now behind them. She was gone from his house and, finally, from his heart. Brian realized he hardly ever thought about her any more, and when he did it was with a growing resentment. Sometimes, he was still able to recall the image of her face. But instead of the sophisticated, stunning woman he fell in love with, now he saw her face when she told him she didn't love him. He saw the way she stood over him, looking down and tossing back her long, blond hair.

Brian preferred to think of Jenny Sullivan. Her image appeared in his mind's eye—Jenny, pretty as Snow White. Jenny poring over the rack of mysteries. Jenny holding a paintbrush and frowning at her own genius.

He looked at his watch. The hardware store was still open. He could probably get in a few hours of painting before bedtime. Brian found his car keys and headed for the door.

"She's gone," he said aloud before he walked out. He was relieved.

Chapter Nineteen

Brian slept well that night and awoke the next morning completely refreshed. He was still sleeping in the guest room, as he hadn't completed painting the master bedroom. He drank an extra cup of coffee on the patio, which made him a few minutes late in opening the bookstore. He knew it would aggravate some of the morning coffee and newspaper crowd, but it was almost worth it. It was a beautiful day.

"Good morning," he said to his customers as he opened the door. "How are you today, folks?"

"It's Friday," one man grumbled. "Don't ever be late with my morning coffee on a Friday again, Brian."

"This won't take long," he promised. "And it's on the house this morning." He hummed while he made the coffee and several of his regulars took notice of his unusually good mood.

"Did you win the lottery?" one asked.

"Nope," he said.

"Pick a lucky horse at the track?"

"I wish."

"Buy a bigger boat?"

"Not a bad idea, but no. I'm just in a good mood today."

"I'll say," one woman said, grinning. "It's not like you to be this chipper, Brian. It looks good on you. Keep it up."

"I'll do that."

He spent the day cleaning the entire store until it shined. Every shelf and counter was polished and dusted. He even redid the display in the front window. He kept the Anna Waters books as the center attraction, of course, but he also worked in a few other titles he thought would be of interest to his clientele—diverse as they were.

Toward the end of the day, Brian began checking his watch. Soon, Jenny would be walking through the door in search of a new mystery. Despite the busywork he made for himself and a steady stream of customers, time started to drag. Finally, a half-hour before closing, she walked in. "Hey," she said.

"Hey, yourself. You're late. That's not like you."

"I know," she said. "It's been one of those days."

"I've been waiting for you."

"Oh?" she asked. "How come? Does the mural need touching up?"

"No," he said. "The mural's perfect. I just like seeing you."

Jenny cocked her head to one side, a curious expression on her face. "I like seeing you too, Brian," she said hesitantly.

Brian caught her eye and held her gaze for several seconds before she glanced at the floor. "The store looks great," she said.

"I've been doing some spring cleaning." Suddenly, he couldn't get enough of looking at her.

She smiled uncomfortably and he forced himself to stop staring. "I'd better find a book so you can get out of here on time," she said. Brian let her go to the mystery section and browse through the books. Tonight, she quickly made a choice and returned to the front register. "I hope I didn't take too long," she said, still smiling sheepishly. "I know you want to close up."

"No," he said. "As a matter of fact, I was hoping that you wouldn't mind waiting around until closing time." It was easy for him to ask the question, and it surprised him. Not that he was shy around women, but it'd been a long time since he'd asked one on a date.

"What's up?" she asked.

"I could use a pepperoni pizza," he told her. "Care to join me?"

Jenny shrugged. "You're singing to the choir. Mario's stays open until eleven."

"Maybe I'll close up a little early tonight."

"There's someone in the science fiction books. Let him take his time. I don't mind waiting."

"Thanks," Brian said. "That would be better. I was ten minutes late in opening this morning."

Her forehead wrinkled. "That's not like you," she said. "Are you feeling all right?"

"I feel great. As a matter of fact, I haven't felt this good in a long time."

They talked about their day while they waited for the last customer. Jenny leaned over the counter confidentially. "Anna hasn't let her sudden success go to her head," she said. "She's still the same old crazy lady we both know and love."

"Incredible, isn't it?" he said. "The sales for *Murder in Orange* are skyrocketing. I've heard talk that there may even be a movie."

"I heard that too, but Anna says it's just a rumor. She has, however, agreed to make a few appearances on some of the television talk shows. One in California and two in New York City. That should be exciting."

"I can't imagine Anna smiling sweetly and making small talk while rubbing elbows with TV celebrities."

"I can't see it either," Jenny said. "But apparently the television people are hoping for anything but sweet smiles and small talk. They think Anna's reputation as a curmudgeon is good for ratings. The crustier she is, the more books she sells and the more the public wants to get to know her. Of course, she says she has no time for all the fuss. She says she's too busy writing *Murder in Red.*"

"Anna's charming when she's plotting murders, isn't she?"

The man from the science fiction section finally appeared at the cash register with a small stack of books, and Brian rang up the sale. He slipped the books into a bag and handed it to his last customer of the day.

"Thank you, sir. Enjoy your books."

"I will," the man said, catching Brian's eye and winking. "You two have a nice evening, young man. It's a lovely night for a romance."

"Thanks," Brian said. "But didn't you just buy a stack of science fiction paperbacks? The romance books are in the back corner near the gazebo."

"I wasn't referring to my evening, young man," the customer said with a nod toward Jenny. "And you might want to think about browsing the romance section yourself."

"Romances are for dreamers," Brian told him, giving Jenny a secret smile.

"Ah, but they're so very sweet," the man said, and then bowed gallantly before sashaying out the door.

Brian shook his head at Jenny and frowned. "Why are all my customers crazy?"

"I don't know," she laughed. "Must be the neighborhood."

"Maybe that's it."

Finally, Brian locked up the store for the night. Not realizing it, he took Jenny's hand in his as they made their way to the restaurant around the corner. When he did realize the bold move he had inadvertently taken, he smiled and squeezed her hand tighter. It felt as if it belonged right where it was.

"Hello, Brian," Mario called, when they walked into the pizza parlor.

"Hey." Being business neighbors, Brian knew Mario well. They often provided each other with change when it ran low, and shared information relevant to their respective business concerns. Brian had once reviewed some contracts for Mario, which took all of an hour to complete. He found some errors that ultimately saved Mario money. In return for the favor, Mario often stopped by the bookstore around lunchtime, bearing sliced submarine sandwiches for whoever happened to be shopping, free of charge.

"Come in, come in," Mario called. "I'll find you a nice table." Within minutes Jenny and Brian were seated in a quiet corner of the restaurant next to a window that overlooked the street.

"I know you," Mario said to Jenny when he handed them the menus. "You're the pretty lady who comes in every Friday and orders a small pepperoni to go."

"Guilty," Jenny said.

"You're driving my waiters crazy," Mario said, leaning close to whisper this confession. "Every Friday, it's the same thing. They hang around the carry-out window, pushing each other and fighting like roosters until you arrive. Peter is the worst of the bunch. He likes you."

"My goodness," Jenny said, blushing. "I had no idea."

"Don't be embarrassed," Mario said. "I can see that you're modest. You really have no idea of the havoc you create among my staff every Friday. I should have expected as much. I've always maintained that a truly beautiful woman is unaware of her beauty."

Jenny's cheeks were turning pinker by the moment. "Thank you," she said.

Mario looked at Brian and shrugged. "And this beautiful woman is living proof of the validity of my theory. I would like to discuss it further with you, Brian, but my work calls." He then bowed graciously and returned to the kitchen.

"There is certainly a lot of bowing going on tonight," Jenny observed.

"I'm just glad that my customers are not the only crazy people around here. Is there a full moon?"

"There must be."

They didn't bother reading the menu and were ready when a waiter with sad brown eyes came to take their order. They ordered a large pepperoni pizza and a pitcher of beer and the waiter slumped away, looking dejected.

"Heartbreaker," Brian accused Jenny after he left.

"I feel terrible," she said, blushing again.

"As you should," Brian teased. "But don't be too hard on him. He's only human. This must happen to you all the time."

"Hardly ever."

"More than you know."

It was the best date of Brian's life.

The thought seemed absurd when it later came to him, but he immediately knew it was true. He'd been on hundreds of dates (especially during his first two years of college), but none like his date with Jenny. She was so pretty, and it was so easy to talk to her. They drank beer from frosty mugs while they waited for the pizza, laughing and joking like the oldest of friends. When the sad-eyed waiter brought their pizza, they ate it and talked some more.

"So," Brian said, warming to the question he'd been

wanting to ask for days. "What's the story with this newspaper reporter? Skip, isn't it?"

"Chip," Jenny said, knowing full well Brian knew his name. "Chip Matthews. We went on a date last week."

"Oh?"

"Yes." She was blushing again. "It was nice. We went to a lovely restaurant downtown. He's a nice, smart guy. I had a good time."

"Oh?"

She shrugged. "I don't know," she said. "I haven't heard from him since." She shrugged again, as if she didn't care, and Brian felt a simultaneous surge of both relief and anger.

"Hmm," he said, finally. There was an expression on Jenny's face that made him want to choose his next words wisely. "Chip Matthews is obviously not as smart as you think he is. And he isn't nice either."

Jenny shrugged yet again and then gracefully changed the subject. "Anna and Luanne have become as thick and thieves, haven't they? I understand Luanne went with her when she did an interview at the radio station last week."

"Yeah. My mother said, and I'm quoting, 'it was a hoot.' In true Anna fashion, she ended up turning the whole thing around and interviewing the interviewer. Luanne said the man was completely red in the face by the time it was over."

They laughed about Anna and Luanne until Jenny had tears running down her cheeks and she could hardly catch her breath. "Those two," she gasped. "They're so . . . *bad!*"

"Pure evil!"

"They've got to be stopped!"

"But no one has the guts to do it."

They were both holding onto their sides from laughter pains when Mario threw them out. "No charge for Brian and the lovely lady," he said. "But my staff wants to go home. Apparently, Peter's heart is broken and it needs to mend."

"I didn't realize it was so late," Brian apologized. Then he threw a wad of money on the table, hoping it would ease Peter's pain, and they left.

"It's early," he said, taking Jenny's hand again. "Would you like to stop by my place for a cup of coffee?" The words burst out of him before he thought them through, but, once said, he didn't regret them.

"Okay," she said.

"Great. Would you mind driving? That is, unless you don't mind riding on the handlebars of my bike."

"Of course," she said, and led him to the powder blue Mustang he'd fallen in love with.

"Can I drive?" he asked.

"No," she said, climbing behind the wheel. "No one drives Linda but me."

Jenny had a slapdash way of driving. She was not reckless in any way that Brian could ascertain because she obeyed the speed limit and traffic signs—barely. She had a way of poring herself behind the steering wheel of the car and a casualness as she drove that Brian found exciting. She took every turn at just a hair less than too fast and stopped for every red light at the last possible inch. She looked at Brian and talked while she drove, unruffled by the traffic and road around her.

"You drive like a maniac," Brian said. "Here, take a left at the corner."

"What do you mean?" Jenny said, squealing wheels as she took the turn. "I'm a great driver. I've never gotten so much as a speeding ticket."

"I don't believe you. Take a right at the light."

"Okay," she said. "There've been six, but that's since high school. I've been behaving myself, though. I haven't gotten a speeding ticket for almost a year. I haven't been in any accidents either."

"That I believe, but how many have you caused? It's the third row house on the right."

"You could have taken your bike home, you know."

"And miss all this excitement? My hair will be gray by the time we . . . You'll have to park on the next street down. All the spaces are gone this time of night."

"There's a spot right there."

"It's too small. You won't have room to . . ."

Within seconds, Jenny somehow parallel parked her car in an incredibly tight place between two enormous SUVs.

"How'd you do that?" Brian asked, genuinely impressed. She shrugged. "No one on this street ever finds a parking space this time of night. That's why I ride a bike to work."

"I told you," she said. "I'm a great driver."

Brian climbed out of the car and led her to his house.

"I'll remember that next time I accuse you of reckless driving," he said, leading her to the house. "Here we are."

"Wow," she said, walking inside. "This is really nice, Brian."

"Thanks."

"I love to explore old houses. Would you mind if I took a look around?"

"Not at all," he said, and led her on a guided tour.

"This is incredible," she said, looking at the high ceilings. "Is this the original plaster?"

"Mostly."

"How about the floors? Original hardwood?"

"Yes, but it took hours of work to restore them. This was a fixer-upper when I bought it. And by fixer-upper, I mean fixer-upper."

"I love it," she said, and Brian knew she was telling the truth.

"I wish my wife thought so," he said, again blurting out something without thinking. Only this time he regretted it.

Jenny smiled, but a line of worry creased her forehead. "Well," she said. "She certainly did a wonderful job decorating the place."

"Not really," he said. "Michelle's tastes lean more toward the ultra-contemporary." Brian quickly changed the subject by telling Jenny about his home improvement efforts. He spoke rapidly, telling her details he thought a draftsman and artist would appreciate. "Here's the master bedroom," he said, finally on the last room. He led her gingerly past the paint cans and ladder. "It's my last project."

She looked around the room. "Nice color."

"Thanks," he said. "I'll be finished by this weekend."

"You have no furniture."

"I've been using the spare bedroom. But I'm ready to move back in."

She looked at him quizzically and finally said, "It's a great house."

"Thanks. How about that cup of coffee?"

He led her back down the steps and into the kitchen and found the can of coffee. "Sorry, all I have are these plastic cups," he said, after he began brewing a fresh pot. "They haven't melted yet, though, so they'll do until I can go shopping."

"I don't mind," Jenny said with a shrug. She watched Brian as he gathered the cups, milk, sugar, and spoons together. When the coffee was finished brewing, he poured some into a thick red plastic mug.

Jenny accepted it and took a sip, looking thoughtful. Brian sensed there was something bothering her. "Let's go in the living room and sit down," he suggested. Once there, she sat on the sofa and he sat down next to her.

"I had a great time tonight," he said, looking into her face.

"I did too."

"I . . . Jenny, I have something I've been wanting to say."

She suddenly stood up. "It's getting late," she said, her face reddening. "I'd better go."

"Why?" he asked, confused. He stood up so that he was standing next to her. "You just got here. Stay awhile."

"Well," she said. "Okay. I guess I should drink the coffee. No harm in that." She sat back down, but she was sitting on the edge of her seat.

"What's wrong?" Brian asked.

"Nothing," she said, smiling primly.

"Oh, no," he said. "Don't do that, Jenny."

"Don't do what?"

"I've had enough problems that stemmed from poor communication. Something's bothering you. Spit it out."

She blushed further. "Okay," she said. "It's just that . . . Look, Brian, I've known you for almost two years now and you've never given me the time of day. I admit, I was attracted to you from the moment I met you at the bookstore, but . . ."

"But, what?" he asked, euphoric.

"But when I found out you were married, I realized my attraction was wrong. All wrong."

"My wife walked out on me months ago," Brian said. It hurt to say the words aloud, especially to Jenny. "She left me after less than a year of marriage. The divorce will be final in two months."

"I know," Jenny said. "Anna told me, and I'm sorry."

He grimaced. "Don't be. It took some time to feel good about my life again, but I'm better now. I see things clearer and I'm on the mend. I'm not going to lie to you, Jenny. I was miserable when she left. I thought I'd never see the light of day again, but . . ."

Jenny put her index finger over his lips. "I understand," she said. "I'm so sorry you went through that. But . . . Brian, I don't date married men. Even men that are almost divorced. It's a little rule I made for myself about eighteen months ago when my boyfriend went back to his wife."

Jenny's confession took Brian by surprise. Eighteen months—that was about the time he'd first met her. "I didn't know he was married," she added quickly. "Not at first. He didn't tell me until we were dating for a few months. I know I should have walked out on him right then and there for lying, but he told me he'd been separated for more than two years. He said he was afraid if I knew about his estranged wife, I wouldn't want to be with him. I didn't find out that he exaggerated his timeline by roughly twenty months. He also forgot to mention his two children. After I found out about them, I realized he was a liar and I could never trust him."

"I'm sorry," Brian said. "I know how much that must have hurt, Jenny. But my situation isn't like that. Michelle left *me* and she isn't coming back. There are no children either. As it turns out, she doesn't really like them."

Jenny blinked at him, her face still troubled and confused. "I'm sorry," she said again.

"Don't be. I've finally reached the conclusion that this has all been for the best."

She said nothing; she only sat looking at him, her eyes searching.

"Jenny?"

"Yes?"

"I won't lie to you."

"I know," she said, almost standing up again, and then she changed her mind and sat back down. "You really aren't like that, are you?"

Then he kissed her.

He held her tightly, falling into the tenderness of her touch, reveling in the feel of her body so close to his. They kissed for a long time, exploring each other's mouths with their tongues. Kisses that were deliciously warm and incredibly soft. He kissed her in a way he'd never kissed anyone else. In a way he'd never kissed Michelle.

"Jenny," he whispered. "You're beautiful and you're . . ."

She looked up at him, her eyes foggy, then the panicked expression returned. "This is happening too fast," she stammered, trying to stand.

"No," he said, pulling her back to him. "It's happening too slowly! I wish I'd met you before. I wish . . ."

Jenny pulled away. She took a deep breath and smoothed down her hair. "I can't believe I was about to break my biggest rule." She stood up before Brian could stop her, picked up her purse and walked to the door. "Brian," she stammered, looking like a deer caught in headlights. "I don't date married men. I'm sorry . . . Call me in two months."

Chapter Twenty

Brian called Jenny the next morning, not because he'd forgotten what she said and not because he'd forgotten the taste of her kisses. He called her to tell her that he'd wait as long as she wanted him to. "But don't go away," he said.

Jenny was as friendly as always. "I'll see you on Friday," she said, after he'd said what he had to say. "We'll talk about it then."

So Brian waited all week for Friday to come and when it finally did, Jenny was, once again, late arriving to the store. Of course, he could have simply called her again. That was what any sane man would have done, and he did pick up the phone a dozen times that day. Maybe he'd invite her out for pizza again. Maybe she would come back to his house. Each time, he hung up the telephone before it had the chance to ring. No, he told himself. It was better to wait until Jenny was ready.

The store was busy, but then again, it was usually busy now. The slow times were further and further apart. Brian recently enlisted one of Travis's friends for help on the weeknights. Hailey ran the cash register and coffee bar while Brian worked around the store. Ever since Anna Waters's latest book became the number one bestselling book in the country (three weeks in a row), and ever since Chip Matthews's glowing article about the store, business was booming. People came from as far as Pennsylvania and New York. Brian was even starting to think about opening up another store.

He walked around with his clipboard, pretending not to appear too anxious every time the door bells jingled. Jenny was late. The bells jingled again and again and each time, Brian would look up from his work to see if it was her and each time, it was someone else.

As usual, Brian busied himself with some small task to take his mind off his thoughts, and was elbow deep in organizing the romance books when she walked in. He barely noticed her, at first. He was re-alphabetizing the books lined up on the painted-on vine-covered shelves near the painted-on gazebo. "What happened to this place?" the hazily familiar voice said from behind him. Brian turned around and almost fell over with surprise—Michelle was standing right in front of him!

She hadn't changed a bit. She was impeccably dressed as always in a baby blue pantsuit with a crisp white blouse. Her hair was somewhat shorter, but not much. It'd always been her crowning glory. She was smiling demurely.

"Hello," he said stiffly, returning to his work.

"Hello, Brian."

"What do you want?"

She was taken aback by the icy tone of his voice and the surprise showed on her face. "What kind of greeting is that?" she said, sticking out her lower lip in a pretty pout. "I'm still your wife, remember?"

"Not for long," he reminded her. "What do you want?"

She tossed her head back and eyed him coolly, no longer bothering with the phony smile. "Well," she said. "If you must know, I stopped by to see the store. Imagine my surprise when the talk of the town in Baltimore is a darling bookstore in Annapolis. *Our* darling book store."

"My bookstore," he corrected her. "You never wanted anything to do with this place, remember?"

"If memory serves me correctly, this little endeavor was a decision we made together—as man and wife— in our short, but oh-so-epic union. I'm entitled to half of everything we purchased together during our marriage, Brian. Or did moldering among the books make you forget all your legal training?"

"You said when you left that I'd get the store and the row house . . ."

"Oh, yes. The row house. That reminds me, I stopped by today and took a look around."

"You broke into my house?"

"Our house," she hissed. "And *my* key still fit the lock. You've been a busy boy, haven't you? I saw all the improvements you made to our little love nest, and I'm impressed. I guess Luanne's acorn hasn't fallen far from the tree. Not really my taste, though. The colors are a bit too bold for me, but you always did like those dark, drab colors, didn't you?"

"I'm changing the locks tomorrow," Brian said.

"That doesn't matter to me. I've seen all I need to see. My realtor friend tells me that with the improvements you've made, the place should sell quickly. It's finally worth more than what we paid for it. I may even walk away with a little bit of money in my pocket from that dump after all."

"I'm not selling my house!"

"You may not have a choice. I don't mind if you buy out my interest, for a reasonable price, of course. What really is going to prove to be profitable, however, isn't the house. The real goldmine is this store. I can't believe it, but it's true. This dirty little bookstore is like a pot of gold . . ."

"It's not dirty!" The anger welled up inside him; he spat out the words one syllable at a time.

"You're right," she said, looking around. Her eyes were hard and cold. "It's as clean as a whistle. Frankly, I can't believe what you've done with the place, Brian. It's lovely."

"What happened to being fair, Michelle?" he snapped. "You took every stick of furniture and cleaned out our bank account, remember?"

"Our *joint* bank account!"

"The store was opened with my savings! You never put in a dime."

"You were always the saver, weren't you? But it was a joint account and, as such, it's considered marital property under the law. I'm entitled to half, Brian. Half of the bank account, half of the house, and half of this store."

"You never wanted anything to do with either the house or the store!"

"I've changed my mind," she hissed. "I'm entitled to it and I deserve it!"

"Deserve it? You wanted me to stay at my father's firm. You wanted to live in a condo near the harbor."

"I deserve every dime I can get my hands on!" her voice was growing louder. "I wasted too much of my time on you! The least you can do is give me my fair share of the money I'm entitled to."

"Money?" Brian said. "Is that all our marriage meant to you?"

"I want what's coming to me. Roger says I should . . ."

"Roger? Who's Roger?"

"Roger Honaker," Michelle looked as if she regretted mentioning her new boyfriend's name. "He's a colleague! You met him. He'd just started working for Simon when you quit to open this cute little shop. He's my friend. I'm allowed to have friends, aren't I? Roger thinks I shouldn't let you and Simon railroad me out of what's rightfully mine. Roger says . . ."

"I could care less what Roger says!" Brian exploded. "You and I took vows to love, honor, and cherish, remember? Doesn't that mean anything to you? Didn't I mean anything to you? How could you let someone tell you what to do? How could you let someone come between us?"

"There isn't any us! There never was!" The words stung him like a slap in the face.

"We had an agreement," Brian said, after a long moment. "You took the furniture and cleaned out the bank account, and I got the mortgage and the bookstore—the two things about our life that you hated the most."

"Neither of which was worth a dime at the time!"

"I made them profitable! I was the one who did the restoration work in the row house and I was the one who put in the twelve-hour days at this store! I worked around the clock so I didn't have to think about you. You didn't leave me with anything else. I made a new life for myself after you walked out!"

"That's not the way I see it," Michelle said, with equal venom. "Nor is it the way the courts will see it. You'll be hearing from my attorney, Brian. His name is Roger Honaker!" With that, she tossed her long, blond hair behind her, turned on her high heels, and stomped away.

Brian looked around the store and saw that his customers were watching. They were hiding behind the bookshelves or huddled at the tables pretending to read. But it was obvious that the ugly shouting match he'd just had with Michelle was overheard by everyone in the store. He felt his face turn red, and he threw up his arms. "Show's over, folks," he called. "I'm sorry to interrupt your shopping."

"Take that witch to court, Brian!" one of the regulars shouted.

"Yeah," said another. "I'll testify that you're the one here every time I walk through the door. I'll tell the judge who made this place great. Who does she think she is?"

Spontaneous applause broke out around the store, echoed by indignant grumblings from the clientele.

"Thanks," he said. "But that won't be necessary. I'm sure we'll work this out like adults. Eventually." The customers reluctantly went back to their shopping and Brian went back to the romance novels.

"Hi," said a voice behind him.

Brian turned, expecting to find that Michelle had returned for round two. Instead, he saw Jenny, looking concerned. "Hi," he said, pasting the best smile he could muster on his face, but he knew he wasn't fooling her. "I'm sorry you saw that."

"I'm sorry you saw it too," she said. "I take it that was Michelle?"

"Yep. That's Michelle all right. Charming, isn't she?"

"I'm sure she has her good qualities," Jenny said. "And I'm sure Simon can take care of any disputes that have arisen . . ."

"I can handle this," he said. The look of worry on Jenny's face made him want to sweep her up into his arms and hold onto her. Instead he stepped back away from her. "I'm a lawyer too, remember? But forget all that. I'm glad you're here. Can you wait for me until I close up? I need to talk to you."

"That's why I stopped by," she said. "I . . . Brian, Chip's waiting for me outside."

His face fell. "Chip?"

"It's not a date or anything," she said, quickly. "He asked me if I would give him a tour of Annapolis. He's writing another article for the newspaper. Suddenly,

Annapolis is the toast of the Mid-Atlantic region. Chip's editor has only given him two days to write it. He's in a bit of a jam. He asked me if I could help him."

"I need to see you."

"I'm sorry. I can't tonight, but . . ."

"Jenny," Brian said. "I wanted to talk."

"I'm sorry to leave you like this, Brian. Call me tomorrow." She kissed him quickly on the cheek. "I still think you need Simon's help. How will you have time to run the store and be a lawyer too?"

"Trust me," he said. "My father doesn't need to know about this. Simon would only start throwing his weight around and end up provoking Michelle."

"But . . ."

"Don't worry," he said. "I'm embarrassed you saw that entire scene, but it doesn't change the way I feel about you. Can't you postpone your tour with Skip? Better yet, can't someone else give him a tour of the city?" Brian knew he sounded jealous, but that was only because he was jealous. Insanely jealous.

"It's Chip," she said. "And, no. I can't; he's waiting for me in the car."

Then Brian said the same two words he'd once said to Michelle. The two words he'd hoped never to say again. "Don't go."

"I have to," Jenny said. "I thought things through last night and I came to a conclusion. I care for you, Brian, probably more than I should. But I don't date married men. I know that sounds cruel, especially in light of the problems you're going through, and this isn't some-thing that's easy to say. I made a promise to myself a long time ago and I won't break it. I'm here to support you, as a friend and as someone who cares, but as far as anything romantic . . ."

"I understand that," Brian said. "And I can wait two more months for you. But I still need to be near you, even if it isn't a romance. I can live with that if that's what you want. Romances are for dreamers, right?"

"What's wrong with being a dreamer?" she asked, and he thought he saw the trace of a smile on her lips.

"Do you really want me to answer that?"

"Yes," she said. "In two months."

He watched her walk away. She moved slowly and once Brian saw her hesitate, as if she was going to turn around and walk back to him, but she didn't. When she got to the door she stopped and looked at him. On her face was an expression of regret that almost broke Brian's heart.

Chapter Twenty-one

Brian called Jenny the next day, and then the next day, and then the day after that. His daily chats with Jenny soon became as normal as brushing his teeth in the morning. They talked about the weather or about the antics of Anna Waters and Luanne McKenzie. Occasionally, but not often, they talked about the legal issues involved in Brian's divorce. They even talked about the tours of Annapolis Jenny provided for Chip Matthews and his newspaper. Anything was an open topic for conversation, except for Brian's growing feelings for her. But he was determined to live up to his promise to her.

"Chip asked me to take him to the murder sites," Jenny said one morning.

"All of them?"

"Yes. All of them."

"How many are there?"

"I counted twenty-three but I was just counting the ones in the Bux McGee series. If we counted all the murders from all of Anna's books, I'm sure it would be considerably more. Maybe fifty."

"That many?"

"Yes. Anna is surprisingly bloodthirsty. It was difficult to plan a tour of the murder sites. I took some notes from the books so I could map out a tour. I didn't want to criss-cross back and forth all over town. Did you know there's been talk of a bus tour doing the exact same thing?"

"No," Brian said. "I didn't hear that one, but I'm not surprised. Anna's books sell out as soon as I get them in. People from all over are coming to my store to buy autographed copies. Anna signs every copy I get in, thanks to my mother. Did you have fun showing Skip around?"

"It's Chip."

"Whatever."

"Yes," Jenny said. "He's really quite charming, in a Baltimore kind of way. Actually, he's from Arizona. He can't believe the humidity here or the hot weather. I showed him where Anna lives—he promised not to put it in the newspaper—and I took him to the street where Bux McGee has an office."

"Where's that?"

"Not far from your store. It's just around the corner. Of course, there's no such address. Anna says she wanted to put Bux on a fictitious street, maybe call it Baker Street, but she changed her mind because that would have been too Sherlock Holmes-ish. The street is real, but the number was made up."

"How's her next novel coming along?" Brian asked. "Anna hasn't been stopping by to listen to my mother's readings as much as she used to. She says she's trying to finish the book."

"I saw her last week and she said she's almost done. She may even be finished by now. Anna says the next one she writes will be the last of the series."

"I hope not. I love Bux. She's not serious, is she?"

"I'm afraid she is. Anna says writing about Bux is growing tedious. She's thinking of starting a new series—one about a middle-aged mother of lawyers who reads to children, makes home repairs, and investigates unsolved homicides."

"She sounds familiar."

"She should."

They laughed. "I miss you," Brian said, his voice dropping.

"But you just saw me yesterday," Jenny replied. "And you'll see me tomorrow."

"I will? What's happening tomorrow?"

"Your mother is having a crab feast. She invited Chip. For some unexplained reason, he's never eaten a crab. Can you imagine? He's been living in Maryland for almost three years!"

"Poor guy," Brian said. "Naturally, my mother has offered to steam him up a few dozen, along with crab cakes, crab salad, crab soup, crab fritters, crab . . ."

"Bingo!" Jenny laughed. "Luanne is going to give Chip a taste of the Chesapeake Bay he'll never forget!"

"I'll bring the mallets," Brian said.

"I'm bringing the coleslaw."

They laughed and said good-bye, but before they hung up, Brian offered one last thought. "I looked at my calendar this morning."

"Oh?"

"Yep. We've only got forty-eight more days to go."

Chapter Twenty-two

"First you break off the legs," Jenny told Chip, leaning closer to get a better view. "Some people wait until after they open the apron to break off the claws, but I like to do them first. Either way is acceptable."

Chip and Jenny were seated, side by side, at a wooden picnic table in the screened-in porch off the back of Simon and Luanne McKenzie's house. Huckleberry lay at Jenny's feet. Luanne gave Brian a long, steady look when Jenny came into the yard and was greeted by a friendly, tail-wagging Huckleberry. A look that was not lost on Brian. The meal was eaten outside, despite the fact that it was hot as an oven on the porch. But crab picking is a messy business that should never come indoors, and there were far too many bugs coming up from the Severn River today to eat under the McKenzies' gazebo. A ceiling fan provided a small blast of warm air that blew down on them while they ate.

Brian eyed Chip Matthews suspiciously from across the table. Ever since he'd walked onto the porch, Brian noticed something that had completely escaped Jenny's attention. Brian could see that Chip Matthews had fallen for Jenny, and fallen for her hard. "Show me again," he said, his brown eyes watching her every move.

"Like this," she said. "Just break them off." She snapped the legs off the crabs and pulled them apart with an experienced hand, revealing the sweet white meat inside. "And, voila! See, now you eat the meat from the claws."

"This whole smashing one's dinner with a mallet is a new one for me," he said.

"You only do that when the meat doesn't come out," Jenny explained. "And you would never want to smash it. You'd have broken shells in your food. Just tap it enough to crack whatever needs cracking. Okay? Next, pull this little tab-like thing down. That's called the apron. Then, break open the bottom, like this . . . See? You don't want to eat the mustard."

"Yuck," Chip said, wrinkling his nose. "I wouldn't dream of it. What is that stuff?"

"You don't want to know. Okay, pull off the devil's fingers. That's those spongy looking things. You don't want to eat those either, although you could."

"Are you sure that we're supposed to eat any part of these horrible creatures?"

"They're delicious," she said. "Now, break it in half, like this . . . Look at all that meat! That's a good one, Chip."

"If you say so."

"Eat it. It taste like lobster, only sweeter."

Chip looked cautiously at the glob of white that was pulled from the inside of the crab. He sniffed it, and then hesitantly put it in his mouth. "Hmm," he said. "It does taste a little like lobster. Not bad, but slimy. Are you sure we don't use forks and knives?"

Anna stared at him coldly from across the table. "The use of utensils would prove to be a most inefficient method of eating a crab, young man. It would also be a sacrilege."

"Sorry," he said, winking at Jenny. "What do I know about seafood? I grew up in the desert."

"I'm very sorry for you," Luanne said. "The Chesapeake Bay has possibly the best seafood in the world. After dinner, I'll show you the crab traps."

"What do you use for bait?" he asked.

"Rotten chicken," Brian said, staring at him.

"Really?" Chip asked.

"Really," Anna said. "The smellier, the better. Crabs love it."

Brian found it difficult to talk to Chip. He didn't like the way Chip looked at Jenny from head to toe when she wasn't watching, as if she were a package he wanted to open. Brian tried to empathize with him, but he couldn't. Brian understood why he was attracted to Jenny and could hardly fault him for those feelings, yet there was something about Chip that Brian didn't like. He was too charming, too smart, and too attractive for Brian to feel anything but acute suspicion whenever he saw him.

Brian looked away and tried to talk himself out of his

jealousy. Instead, he chatted with Anna's husband Frank and watched the sun move slowly down the sky. The day was finally cooling off as the last of the crabs were cracked open and eaten. They'd already polished off the crab salad and crab fritters. Luanne did not bring out the crab soup for fear the diners would melt from the added heat. Simon provided a cooler full of cold sodas and beer, and he kept replenishing everyone's beverages. They drank right from the bottles with dirty hands and didn't mind the grime that formed on the glass.

"Not the cleanest meal I've eaten," Chip confessed, wiping his hands with a paper towel. "And it's a lot of work for a little bit of food, but it was probably the best meal I've had in quite some time."

"Congratulations," Frank said. "You're officially a resident of Maryland."

"Thanks. Next time, I'll give you a taste of my home town. I'll bring the lizard stew."

"Oh, my!" Luanne gasped. "Do you really eat lizards in Arizona?"

"Not at my house," he said. "But I bet I could make you the hottest cheese dip you've ever eaten."

"I'm game," said Simon.

"Let's plan on it," Chip said. "Next week? I'd invite you all to Baltimore, but my apartment isn't very big and . . ."

"Same time, same place next Sunday," Simon said. "And thank you, young man. But I never go to Baltimore unless I'm suing someone." He gave Brian a hard look.

They talked about nothing for the next hour until the bugs somehow managed to squeeze their way through their screened fortress. "Ouch!" Simon growled, swatting at yet another mosquito. "I think someone is trying to tell us something. We'd better take this party inside, folks. Unless you want to be eaten alive!" They'd already tossed the crab shells into a large plastic garbage bag. All that was left to do was dump out the ice from the cooler and head back in.

"I wish we could stay," Chip said. "But I have to get back to Baltimore. Jenny promised to show me the marina at night. We'd better go before it closes. Thank you for an . . . interesting dining experience."

"Thank you," Luanne said. "I'm proud to say that now you can pick a crab with the best of them."

They all grabbed whatever remained of the debris and headed into the house. Brian followed closely behind Chip and Jenny as they went into the kitchen, and he watched them as they washed up at the sink. "You're a mess!" Chip laughed, patting her cheek with his still-dirty hand.

"You are too," she laughed.

Brian felt, for a fleeting instant, as if he'd walked in on two lovers, and considered slamming Chip to the floor. Of course, he reconsidered and washed up instead.

"Ready to go?" Chip asked Jenny, taking her hand.

She untwined her hand from his, but did it with a smile. "Yes," she said. "We should go before it gets too dark." They said their good-byes to everyone and headed for the door.

"I'll walk you out," Brian said, still following behind them. Watching Jenny leave with Chip weighed heavily on him as they walked toward the driveway. He wanted to be alone with her. He wanted to pick up her hand, just like he did when they walked to Mario's.

The night was alive. The sky was turning to hazy shades of pink and purple and the creature population from the river was noisily chirping and croaking and hissing. Jenny sighed. "It's so pretty," she said.

"You're so pretty," Chip said, forgetting that Brian was behind them. He looked at her boldly, and she blushed and said nothing.

Brian again fought the urge to do Chip bodily harm—perhaps throwing him into the river that ran behind his parents' house. Instead he shook Chip's hand once he'd unlocked the door to his shiny red sports car. "Thanks for everything," Chip said after he tucked Jenny into the front seat.

There was a look in his eye that Brian couldn't quite identify, but the meaning became clearer as he shut the car door. There was a swagger in his walk and a look of triumph on his face. "You didn't need to escort us," Chip said, his voice low. "We can figure things out on our own."

"No problem," Brian said.

Chip eyed him steadily and Brian returned the gaze until they were glaring at each other. "She won't wait for you, you know," Chip said.

"What do you mean by that?"

"You know exactly what I mean. A woman like that doesn't have to wait for anyone."

Chip then turned and walked back to the car. He started the engine, still staring at Brian, and quickly pealed out of the driveway with a spray of gravel.

"Oh, yeah?" Brian said to the taillights of the car. "It's only forty-seven days."

"Brian McKenzie?"

The voice came out of the shadows and surprised Brian so much he almost fell over.

"Who are you? Who's there?"

"I'm Roger Honaker," the voice said, and a large, boxy man stepped into the light from out of the shadows.

"Who?"

"Roger Honaker. I'm the attorney for Michelle McKenzie."

Brian looked at him in the dim light. He was taller than Brian by several inches, and everything about him seemed to be square. His body was square, and his jaw; even his closely-trimmed dark hair had a four-sided quality to it.

"What the hell are you doing in my parents' driveway this time of night?" For the second time in what seemed like mere minutes, Brian fought the urge to throw a man into the river. Except, in the case of Roger Honaker, he had to dig his fingers into the palms of his hands to keep from acting on the impulse.

"I represent Michelle McKenzie," he said again. "She told me you might be here."

Brian couldn't remember ever meeting this man, although Michelle had informed him that Roger once worked with him at Simon's firm. The notion that Brian had met Roger Honaker and forgotten him seemed improbable, however. How could he have forgotten a man shaped like a box? Especially this man.

Brian hated him.

He hated Roger's tall, square bodybuilder physique. He hated his perfectly styled square hair and his chiseled square cleft chin. But mostly, he hated the haughty, superior glint in his dark eyes. "I asked you a question," Brian snarled. "What are you doing here?"

"I'm here on behalf of Ms. Michelle McKenzie," Roger said, taken aback. The man in front of him was much angrier than Roger had anticipated. Brian moved toward him menacingly and Roger stepped back, holding out a thick yellow envelope.

It was almost dark now, but Brian could see well enough to make out that Roger Honaker, just like Chip Matthews, had a sneer on his face. "Your divorce papers," he said, keeping a safe distance between them. "You should take note that there've been a few revisions since the separation agreement."

"Get out!"

For a second, it seemed as if Roger Honaker was going to do just that, but then he squared his square body and said, "By the looks of that young lady who just drove off in that guy's sports car, I suspect you're as eager to move on with your life as Mrs. McKenzie is." Brian glared at him and moved closer.

"I suggest you sign those papers and return them as quickly as possible," Roger said, swallowing hard. "Ms. McKenzie doesn't want to have things drag on for months, even years, any more than you do."

"I said get out!" Brian lunged at Roger but, for a boxed-shape man, he moved surprisingly quickly. He was down the driveway before Brian could grab him and punch him in his smirking, square face.

Chapter Twenty-three

"So, when would be a good time?" Luanne asked her sullen son.

"I don't know, Mom. Just not now."

Luanne McKenzie eyed him curiously. She couldn't put her finger on the problem, but there was something bothering Brian. He was distracted and quiet. He was also eyeing the murals on the walls of the bookstore with a decidedly grim expression.

"I don't understand," she pressed. "A week ago, you couldn't wait to open a second store. Now, you won't even discuss it."

"It's not a good time."

It was clear Brian had said all he was going to say. He knew all too well the dangers of providing his mother with too much information. The last thing he wanted to tell her about was the divorce papers that had recently been handed to him.

"Is it Jenny?"

"No!"

"If I were you, I wouldn't worry about that Chip What's His Name. He isn't our Jenny's type in any way, shape, or form. I also have a sneaking suspicion that he's a playboy, although I can't tell you why I think so. The dog was none too impressed either. Did you notice how Huckleberry's lip curled at him? There's something deceitful about that man."

"Mom," Brian sighed, wearing the same reproachful, know-it-all expression she remembered so well from his teen years. "I have no idea what you're talking about. Huckleberry was a perfect gentleman, and Jenny and I are friends. Just friends."

"Brian, I've seen the way you look at her and the way she looks at you . . ."

"I'm married, remember?"

Luanne winced. "Not for long."

"I don't know how long it will be and neither do you, and I can't ask Jenny to wait. She's a warm, beautiful woman and I'd be an idiot if I thought no one else noticed. I can't expect her to wait around for me, now can I?"

Brian was quoting Simon, never a good sign, and Luanne wondered what had happened to set him off. "Even if the one who notices her is an arrogant reporter?"

Brian didn't have time to respond to that remark because just then the front door opened and in walked Anna Waters. She strode in, with her usual quick, determined stride, her head slightly down and her mouth drawn in a tight frown. "Good morning," she said her voice biting. "Got any coffee?"

"For someone who writes novels as a means of occupation and financial remuneration, you certainly have a limited vocabulary," Luanne scolded.

"Pardon me," Anna said. "Please allow me to rephrase my question: May I inquire as to the existence of a vessel containing a dark brown, aromatic beverage made from ground and roasted beans frequently found in South American shrubbery?"

"That's better," Luanne said, and poured Anna a cup of black coffee.

"Good morning, Anna," Brian said, momentarily forgetting his demons. He'd grown very fond of the writer over the past few months, and her presence always brought a smile to his face. "How's it going?"

"Very well," she said. "Oh, bother! Who am I kidding? I walked into town so I wouldn't have to look at that stupid computer screen for another minute!"

"What's wrong?" Luanne asked.

"I don't know . . . It's just that I'm stuck on the last chapter of *Murder in Brown*."

"It isn't like you to have writer's block," Luanne said.

"I wouldn't exactly call it writer's block, Lu. It's more like writer's tedium. It's just that I've been churning out one book after another after another after another. As soon as I turn one over, my editor has the galleys ready from another! I hate to admit it, but I'm getting a little tired of Bux McGee."

"Tired of Bux?"

"Yes. Don't get me wrong—I love the old coot, but

he can be pig-headed and, frankly, a little bit dense. I mean, how many clues do I have to lay out for him? I'm on chapter eighteen and he still hasn't figured out that Lady Brownell is hiding something. And he's fallen in love with the primary suspect—*again*! Didn't he learn his lesson after that ugly business with the ballerina? He should know better!"

Brian's eyebrow shot up. "Don't mind me for asking silly questions, Anna, but aren't you the one who determines Bux's fate?"

"You obviously know nothing about the writing process," Anna shot back impatiently. "My characters are living, breathing beings, Brian, and they do what they must in order for the story to unfold. But they aren't perfect. Far from it! All too often, they exercise bad behavior and make poor decisions and there's nothing I can do to stop them."

"But . . . Never mind. I think I hear the phone ringing. Would you ladies excuse me?" Brian gave his mother a secret look and quickly exited to his office.

"Now look what I did," Anna groaned to her friend. "Brian thinks I'm off my rocker."

"I can't imagine why," Luanne said.

"I know, I know. But you have no idea how monotonous it can be writing about the same man, day after day! It's like I'm married to him. I would have ended the Bux McGee series two novels ago if it wasn't for my editor. Don't tell anyone I said this, Lu, but there are times when I wish *Murder in Orange* had never become a best seller."

"Anna! *Murder in Orange* made you famous. And rich—not that money matters to crazy people."

"I know, and you're wrong. Money does matter to crazy people. How do you think we get this way? Besides, *Murder in Orange* introduced me to Brian and you, and where would I have to walk to if I didn't have this bookstore? It's just that I don't love Bux in the same way I used to. The spark is gone. We've had a good run, but it's over. I want a divorce."

"You're kidding?"

"No, I'm not kidding. I'll write one last novel, of course. I already have the plot laid out. I just need to decide if I'm going to kill Bux or not. I'd hate to end things on a sour note but, heaven knows, the man has it coming!"

"Anna, no! Don't you dare kill Bux!"

"Oh, but I want to. It would be my pleasure."

"No! You'll do no such thing!"

"Please?"

"*No!*"

"Very well then, I won't kill him. But I can't promise a happy ending."

"Anna Waters!" Luanne snapped. "I cannot and I will not allow you to orchestrate a bad end for Bux McGee. He's been too good to you and he deserves better! I know he has his flaws, dear, but he's still a good man and he's a darn good detective. He's earned his happy ending. I insist that you see to it that he has one."

"Oh, all right. But I'm only doing this as a personal favor to you. Bux will solve one more case and then he'll open up that charter fishing boat business he's always wanted."

"And solve crimes in his free time?"

"No. I never want to see him again."

"I'd leave that door open if I were you. You may find that you miss old Bux after a while."

"Very well, Luanne. I'll revisit the question of future detective work for Bux McGee at another time in the distant, distant future."

"How about a lady friend? Bux does need to get out more."

"Which one?" Anna asked. "The ballerina or the blues singer?"

"How about someone new? Someone with no colorful undertones?"

"Very well. Have it your way. I can hook up Bux with the lady who works in the crime lab and teaches yoga classes. Would that make you happy?"

Luanne eyed Anna triumphantly. "Yes," she said. "As a matter of fact, it does. I'm particularly pleased that I protected you from making a decision you'll regret later. I want to see the draft of this book before you send it to your editor—just in case you change your mind about killing Bux."

"Agreed."

"Promise?"

"I promise. Bux will have his happy ending." Anna sighed, walked behind the coffee bar, and helped herself to another cup of coffee, stealing peeks at the closed office door. "Speaking of happy endings, what's happening with Brian and Jenny?"

"I know as much as you do," Luanne said. "You saw him after he walked Jenny and Chip to the car. He looked furious! And what was that yellow envelope he was carrying?"

"I don't know," Anna said. "All I know is that I heard voices in the driveway after I heard the reporter's car pull away. Obviously, someone else was out there that night. But who could it have been?"

"You're the mystery writer. This should be simple for a mastermind such as yourself."

"Hmpf," she snorted. "You read too many books."

"Get on it, Anna," Luanne said. "This is my son we're talking about. I need to know what was in that envelope and I need to know why he's suddenly decided against opening a new store. I suspect Michelle is behind all this."

"We also need to know a little bit more about young Chip Matthews."

"Right. If our two dunderheads continue to refuse to see that they've fallen in love with each other, then we have no choice but to take matters into our own hands."

"Absolutely," Anna echoed. "They need to be pointed in the right direction."

"It's for their own good."

"Without any meddling, of course."

"Of course," Luanne said. "We'd never do anything like that."

"So then, it's agreed. We need to find out who was in your driveway last Saturday and what was in that yellow envelope. And we need to learn what lurks behind the charming smile of the handsome newspaper reporter."

"What are we waiting for?" Luanne said. "Let's get to it."

Chapter Twenty-four

Brian didn't know what was wrong with his mother. At first he dismissed her odd behavior as the same old routine eccentricities that made her legend, but then Anna started to demonstrate similar quirks. They whispered furtively together in between Luanne's readings to the children when Anna dropped by "just to say hello." The once noisy and often belligerent conversations the two women shared at the table near the coffee bar became much quieter and more clandestine. Sometimes they would "take a walk" around the busy block, or they'd hide behind a bookshelf and speak softly together. If Brian happened upon them, they would clam up with guilty expressions on their faces.

Jenny didn't know what to make of their odd behavior either. She'd long finished painting the murals in the bookstore and her visits were now limited to Friday night purchases of a mystery novel to go along with her pepperoni pizza. Of course, there was the occasional cook-out in Simon and Luanne's backyard and daily phone conversations, but it was all too infrequent for Brian. He wanted to see her every minute of every day. His first thoughts in the mornings when he awoke were of Jenny, and his last thoughts at night before he fell asleep were of her too.

But the sight of her drove him crazy. He wanted to reach out and touch her. Just the scent of her long, dark hair when he stood next to her brought back a flood of delicious memories. He remembered the way her body felt when he held her and remembered the sweetness of her kisses. Instead, Brian settled for their daily telephone conversations and her weekly visit to the store.

"I don't know what they're up to," Jenny said one Friday, after she'd selected a new mystery novel. "Last week, I stopped by Anna's house to show her the cover artwork for *Murder in Green* and I caught the two of them at the kitchen table poring over a notebook. Anna acted like I'd caught them plotting a bank heist."

"I know," Brian said. "They're up to something. Has Anna been asking you a lot of questions lately?"

"Yes," Jenny said. "She's been asking me questions about . . . Chip."

"Oh?" Brian asked. Chip Matthews was becoming an increasingly sore point between them. Jenny would see him occasionally but she insisted that it was all business related, a fairy-tale that Brian suspected Jenny believed, but he wasn't so sure about Chip. Lately, they'd both found it better not mention him at all.

"I've been meaning to ask you about Skip, myself."

"Brian, his name is Chip and you know it."

"Whatever. How is Chip?"

"I wouldn't know. I haven't seen him since I took him to Kent Island for the article he's writing about some of the local sights . . ."

"Whatever happened to the article he was supposed to write in two days?" Brian asked. "I read the newspaper every day and I have yet to see it."

"He's still working on it," Jenny told him. "His editor wanted him to expand the story."

"Uh-huh."

"It's true."

"It's taking a long time to write, isn't it?" Brian asked. "And he seems to have limited his informants to just one."

"Oh, stop," Jenny said. "Chip is doing a biography on Anna."

"So, why doesn't he talk to her?"

"He is. We've all gone out to dinner and to the movies." Her words lingered in the air.

"And?"

"And nothing. We're not dating, if that's what you're asking me."

"I was," he said. "Although I know I don't have a right to."

"Brian," she said, her voice dropping. "Chip has always been a perfect gentleman. He's attentive and sweet. He sends flowers to my office and opens the car door for me. But . . ."

"But?" Brian knew he was making her uncomfortable, but he couldn't help it.

"I don't know," she muttered. "There's something odd about him that I can't put my finger on. He'll want to meet for one reason or another four days in a row, and then he'll disappear for a week. Of course, his boss gives him difficult assignments and he works under a terrible deadline. Look, Brian, can we talk about something else? You have relationship woes of your own to contend with."

Brian grimaced. His relationship troubles were building like a storm coming off the Chesapeake Bay. First, the ominous visit from Roger Honaker in his parents' driveway. And then the phone call came. "I'm taking care of it," he said. His "honesty is the best policy" resolution was quickly fading. The thought of telling Jenny about the latest chapter in the Michelle saga was too disheartening to think about. So he changed the subject. "Did Anna finish *Murder in Brown*?"

"Yes and she's already started the next one. Or should I say the last one. She's calling it *Murder in Paisley*."

"I like the title, but I'm sorry to see Bux go."

"You and a million fans," Jenny said. "Anna's publisher is already issuing press releases. This one could be the biggest-selling novel in her career. Luanne thinks she'll change her mind and write another Bux book in a couple of years."

"You never know," Brian said. He tried to concentrate on Anna, but all he could see was Jenny. "Let's go for a pizza," he said. "I'll chase everyone out and close up the store a few minutes early."

"Maybe," she said, and it surprised him. "How many more days do we have?"

"Eight, but I don't know if it's going to happen on schedule." He watched her face intently and she returned the gaze. Finally she shrugged.

"What's a pizza between friends?"

"Give me ten minutes," Brian said before she could change her mind. "Closing time," he shouted to the far from empty store.

Chapter Twenty-five

It was as if Mario had been waiting for them to arrive. "I already told the kitchen to make a pepperoni pizza," he laughed. "I had a feeling at least one of you two would show up here tonight. Step right this way, Brian and Jenny." Then he led them to a nice quiet table by the window where they could look out over the still bustling Annapolis street.

"This is wonderful, Mario," Jenny said, giving him a winning smile. "Thank you so much."

"Thanks, Mario," Brian echoed.

"Would you like a beverage?"

"Beer?" Brian asked Jenny and she nodded.

"Beer it is," Mario said with a dramatic bow before he headed back to the kitchen.

They made small talk while they waited for their drinks. "This is the first time I've had all day to relax," Jenny said.

"Busy day?"

"Yes, it was." Just then Mario came with a frosty pitcher of beer. He placed it in the middle of the table and then slapped down two beer mugs. "Thank you," she said. "How about you, Brian? I bet today was busy for you too."

"Yes, but lately all of my days have been busy ones. Not that I'm complaining. I'm very happy with the way things have been going for my store lately. It's all thanks to Anna and you."

"Mostly Anna."

"No," he said. "I can't give her all the credit, nor do I think she'd take it. I have just as many people show up for the atmosphere as the books. The murals are unique. You'd be surprised by the number of people who come in with sketch pads and try to replicate your work. Of course, none of them can come close."

Jenny smiled, her cheeks turning that sweet pink again. "Thanks," she said. "But it's me who should be thanking you. I love doing murals more than anything else. Ever since I painted the bookstore, I've had more work than I can handle. I'm already booked for the next six months."

"Really?" Brian's face split into a grin. "Wow! No kidding? I'm happy about that. And I hate to say it, but we probably owe Chip-Skip some of the credit. After all, he was the one who wrote the newspaper article that started it all."

"Yes, he did. So we should give him some of the credit."

"We should," Brian allowed. "Even though I hate, loathe, and despise him."

"Yes, even though you hate, loathe, and despise him." Jenny looked at Brian cautiously, but was relieved to see that he was smiling.

"I don't care about Chip-Skip," Brian said, warming to the new nickname. "Because I'm with you tonight. I'm with you and he's nowhere around and in eight days, I'm going to do everything in my power to see more of you."

Jenny grinned. "Oh, yeah?"

"Yeah," Brian said and picked up her hand. "I adore you," he said, looking into her eyes. "You're beautiful and sweet and brilliant. You're everything I could ever wish for in a woman, and I would consider myself the luckiest man in the world if you would see me. Just me. Only me."

Jenny didn't pull her hand away; instead, she listened to his words with rapt attention. Her eyes were soft and there was a hint of a smile on her lips. "In eight days," she said.

"I don't know if I can wait eight days," Brian said, and he didn't. Just looking at her was making him feel as if he was going to jump out of his skin.

"Your pizza," Mario said, setting the big round pan on their table personally. "Enjoy."

"Thank you, Mario," Jenny said, and busied herself serving their slices onto the plates. "Doesn't this look yummy?" she asked Brian.

"Yes," he said, not taking his eyes off her.

Later, after they'd eaten all the pizza, they decided to take a walk. Brian paid the check, making sure to tip Mario generously, and helped Jenny with her jacket. They stepped out into the cool darkness and Brian took her hand. He loved the way Jenny's hand felt in his, and was surprised by how good it felt. How perfectly it fit into his. It felt as if he'd been waiting his whole life to hold her soft, beautiful hand in his.

They walked toward the harbor, enjoying the crisp, salty air, and talked pleasantly as they walked along the busy streets. Annapolis was a small city, but it was a city with a nightlife all its own. The sidewalks were crowded with people and the shops and restaurants were doing a brisk business.

Once at the harbor, they stopped and bought ice cream cones and ate them as they walked along the dock and looked at the boats, all the while still holding hands. It was a perfect evening. It was warm, but not too much so, and the stars were bright in the sky. They could hear jazz music coming from one of the restaurants. They finished the last of their ice cream and threw a little cone in the water for the gulls. Then they found an empty bench and sat down. Brian put his arm around her and she nestled against him.

"This is nice," she said. He looked into her face to reply but found that he couldn't find the words. She was so beautiful snuggled against him, her eyes bright and her voice lilting. It was a good thing they were sitting down because Brian's legs suddenly felt like rubber. He reached out and touched her chin and brought her face to him. Then his mouth found hers, tasting her deliciousness. At first it was a sweet kiss—gentle and soft, but he wanted more. He feasted on her kisses, and she was kissing him back. He wrapped her around him tighter, hungry and passionate, kissing her lips and her throat and the back of her neck.

She came up for air once and looked around to see if anyone was watching. When she saw that there was no one around, she put her arm around his neck and kissed him again. They stayed on the bench kissing for a long time. Both had lost all track of time and place. They only wanted to kiss and hold each other. She gasped softly when he kissed her in the soft spot right below her ear, and she was trembling.

"Jenny," he moaned. "Oh, Jenny . . ."

Hearing the words he whispered in her ear seemed to bring her back to reality. "Brian," she whispered back, pulling away from him. "We shouldn't." She untangled herself from him and looked into his face. "We . . . better get back," she said, smoothing her hair.

"Why?" he said, reaching for her again.

She smiled at him but stood up, looking around the pier for spies. "Come on," she said. "It's only eight more days." She started back toward the road and Brian reluctantly followed her, trying desperately to think of a way to make those eight days go by faster.

Chapter Twenty-six

Anna Waters and Luanne McKenzie walked into the restaurant in downtown Baltimore.

"May I help you?" the hostess asked, taking in Anna's unruly red hair and dirty sneakers.

"Yes," Anna said. "We're meeting our antagonist here. I'm not sure if she's arrived yet."

"I'll check the reservations. Name please?"

"McKenzie," Luanne said. "Michelle McKenzie."

"No," the hostess said. "There's no McKenzie here . . . No, wait a minute. It's here. Michelle Wellman, with 'McKenzie' in parentheses. Follow me."

The hostess led Anna and Luanne to a table near the window, where Michelle was waiting.

"What's she doing here?" Michelle asked, coldly glaring at Luanne. "I thought this was going to be a private meeting."

"I don't drive, remember?" Anna said, ignoring the

accusatory tone in the young woman's voice. "Luanne was kind enough to provide transportation."

"You're late."

"Traffic was heavy," Luanne said, returning Michelle's scowl with one of her own.

The two of them locked eyes in a staring contest until Michelle finally flipped her long, blond hair and sniffed. "Very well," she said. "Now that the formalities are out of the way, let's begin. Do you have the contract?"

"Yes," Anna said, handing her two sheets of paper. "And I've had my attorney look it over as well."

"Simon McKenzie, no doubt?"

"No. Another firm was retained to handle these negotiations. Frank Monson is the attorney."

"Never heard of him."

"He's quite experienced in contract negotiations."

"This isn't open to negotiation," Michelle said. "I know the law and I intend to fully exercise my rights. Got it?"

"Now wait just one minute!" Luanne snapped. "If you think that you can bully my friend into . . ."

"Luanne," Anna interrupted. "Let me handle this." She turned and leveled her sharp green eyes at Michelle. "Now you listen to me, young lady, and you listen well. My negotiations with you have nothing whatsoever to do with any of your other legal matters. Furthermore, it is unwise to attempt to use me as leverage in your divorce proceedings. Also, you should understand that while it is true I'm friends with the McKenzie family, I consider my dealings with you to be a business transaction between you and me. Everything else is between you and Brian. Understood?" Michelle nodded. "Furthermore, while I am willing to purchase your interest in Brian's Books & Coffee Shop, I am not willing, nor do I intend to, be coerced into signing a contract that isn't in my best interest. You should also know that while my good friend's son has an emotional and financial interest in the outcome of our dealings, I do not. Make no mistake, as far as I'm concerned, our meeting here today is strictly business. To put it to you simply, Ms. McKenzie, I would like to buy your interest in the bookstore. However, you should know before we get down to our discussion that I am not one to fiddle around with negotiations. We need to come to a meeting of minds today."

"So you're not here for Brian?"

"Heavens, no." Anna said. "He's a big boy. He can take care of himself."

Michelle eyed her suspiciously. "What about her?" she said, nodding toward Luanne.

"I'm his mother," Luanne said crossly. "But I'm not going to interfere with his personal business. He'll be along in a few minutes to talk to you."

"Brian's coming here!" Michelle said. "He should go through my attorney."

"You're an attorney," Luanne reminded her. "As is Brian. Surely two attorneys can negotiate a simple divorce."

Michelle looked at her steadily. "All right," she said. "I'm in as much of a hurry to get this over with as he is. I heard all about his new girlfriend. I hear she's rather plain."

"Plain?" Anna said. "She's prettier than you'll ever be, my dear."

Michelle leveled a glare in her direction, then smirked. "Of course she is."

"Can we get back to the matter at hand?" Anna said, drumming her fingers on the table. "I don't have much time. If you don't mind, the contract . . ."

Michelle picked up the papers and read them, scowling. "I need time to read this through."

"I'll give you fifteen minutes," Anna said dryly. "It's only two pages and it's very straightforward. Sign it, or don't sign it. It doesn't matter to me. After that, Luanne and I are walking out the door."

"The service here is atrocious," Luanne said, turning to Anna. "I know of a lovely place in Little Italy. We should try there."

"What if I don't agree to the terms of this," Michelle said, looking up from the papers. "What if I want to negotiate?"

"Take it or leave it," Anna said. "This is the only offer you'll get from me."

Michelle read the contract, occasionally looking at Luanne, who was sipping from a water glass and looking around for the waiter. Exactly fifteen minutes later, Michelle was still poring over the papers in front of her. Anna looked at her watch.

"I'll just leave some money on the table," she said, picking up her handbag. "How much do we owe? We just had water."

"I ordered an iced tea," Luanne said. "But he still hasn't brought it." She slipped a five dollar bill on the table and stood up. Anna stood up as well and the two prepared to walk away.

"Wait," Michelle said. "I'm not finished reading this, and I don't sign contracts under the gun."

"Really?" Anna said. "And I specifically requested that they use small words."

"I could argue duress later," she said.

"There's been no duress from me, my dear," Anna said. "And Luanne is a witness. Besides, we've been in discussion about this matter for a week now. I've made my requirements quite clear. You've had adequate time to come to a decision."

Just then Brian walked into the restaurant and headed for the table.

"Very well," Michelle said, grimly. "I'll sign it." She picked up a pen and scribbled her signature. "Now what?"

"Thanks a bunch," Anna said, just as Brian arrived at the table. "I see that your next conference has arrived, so Luanne and I will be taking our leave. Luanne?"

"Thank you, Anna. Michelle, please send my regards to your parents for me." Luanne stood up and smoothed her skirt, smiling at Brian as she did. "Hello, Brian. Nice to see you, dear."

"Hey, Mom," Brian said, kissing his mother on the cheek. "Anna. Aren't you two staying for lunch?"

"Heavens, no," Luanne said. "The service is poor. I know a place in Little Italy that's lovely. I'd love to go there while I'm in town." She waved a quick goodbye to Brian and nodded at Michelle.

"Does this Italian restaurant have seafood dishes?" Anna asked Luanne as they headed for the door.

"Of course," Luanne said. "It's just a few blocks from here. Let's walk. We can come back for the car."

Brian watched them go with a look of patient benevolence on his face.

"I almost miss Luanne," Michelle said, shaking her head. "Although I suspect the other one isn't playing with a full deck. I wasn't sure if she was bluffing or not."

"She doesn't bluff," Brian said. "But let's just stick to our legal issues, shall we?"

"Very well then," she said, looking him in the eye for the first time since he'd arrived. "I'm not going to mince words, Brian. I have a feeling you want this divorce as much as I do, so let's cut to the chase. I want . . ."

"I want you to sign a quitclaim to the house," Brian said. "That will wrap up everything between us."

"I want half of the proceeds of a sale."

"There isn't going to be a sale, Michelle. I'm keeping the house."

"But . . ."

"No buts."

"We don't have a pre-nup, Bri, remember?"

"It doesn't matter."

"I'm entitled to half," she said, with a shrug. "Sorry, but that's the rule. We bought the house during our marriage. That makes it marital property."

"Yes," Brian said. "But there hasn't been a profit. In

fact, I'm in the hole, what with all the money I've spent to make the restorations. I've kept excellent records of the bills. You're entitled to half of them as well."

Michelle looked at him, none too pleased with this latest bit of news.

"What did you expect? It hasn't been two years since we bought it. Are you taking into account real estate fees? That will probably run in the . . ."

"Never mind," Michelle said tartly.

"I also took the liberty of preparing revised divorce papers," he said, pulling open a folder from his briefcase.

She flipped through the papers he handed her. "I don't know," she said. "I'd like to have my attorney read through these before I sign anything."

"Michelle," Brian said, his jaw a hard line. "You told me that you wanted to be fair. Now it's time for you to do just that."

She looked at him, her green eyes cool and steady for a long moment. Then she looked away. "Where is that waiter?" she sighed. "I hate to say it, but your nutty mother was right. The service here is hideous."

"Michelle," Brian said again. "Sign the papers. Let's put an end to this."

She looked at him again, only this time her eyes were not as steady. This time he thought he saw something more there. Sadness? Regret? Brian wasn't sure what it was because the look was gone in an instant. "Okay, okay," she said, picking up the pen. "I'll sign it."

Chapter Twenty-seven

"Did she sign the divorce papers?" Luanne asked as soon as Brian arrived at the restaurant. He didn't answer, but he smiled and gave her a thumbs-up.

On a hunch, he'd headed for Little Italy in search of Luanne and Anna and found them at the first restaurant he looked in. "She was perfectly reasonable," he said. "How did your meeting go, Anna?"

"Great, partner," Anna said. "I was bluffing, of course. Michelle didn't know it, but our meeting was more my way of testing the waters. I had no idea Michelle would agree to my terms, but Luanne and I thought it was worth a try."

"Worth a try," Luanne echoed.

"I'm glad you suggested it, Brian," Anna said. "Imagine, me the co-owner of Brian's Books & Café. It's just what I needed. I told my husband I was going buggers hanging out around the house every day."

"She was always hanging around the bookstore any-way," Luanne chimed in. "She might as well make herself useful while she's there."

Anna gave her a cool look and said to Brian, "If I have to type the word 'Bux' one more time I'm going to scream! My husband said I needed to find a diversion. I like books, so . . . Well, it was a brilliant idea, Brian, simply brilliant."

"I'm so glad you came to us," Luanne said. "This will work out famously. Despite Anna's advanced years, she's still quite spry."

"Advanced years?" Anna said, shooting her an evil look. "Speak for yourself."

"You're one hundred if you're a day."

"We can discuss our ages later," Anna quipped. "Right now let me talk to Brian."

"Hmpf."

"Brian," Anna continued. "If you don't mind, I would like to have a small room in the back of the new store. I already have a good computer, but I insist that there be a window or two. Other than that, I'm fairly easy to please. The only thing I ask is that it not be in a mall. I despise malls. And I'll need a quiet room for when I want to do my writing. Of course, Jenny will paint a mural for me for inspiration."

"After she does the artwork on the walls of the store," Luanne added. "I want a picture of Huckleberry included in the artwork."

"Of course. Maybe we will have a different theme. Maybe a mountain range or a dude ranch."

"What are you talking about?" Luanne snapped. "We

live in Maryland. The mural's theme will relate to the Chesapeake Bay!"

"Very well," Anna said, nodding.

"Anna will write for a few hours in the morning while I run things in the store."

"Then I'll come out and schmooze with the customers."

"We'll probably have to hire an assistant later on. I still have to keep up with my house and Anna still has to do her book tours and talk shows."

"I'll sign all the copies of my books and have impromptu readings," Anna added. "Just like always."

"And I'll still read to the children for you in your store."

Brian looked at the two of them, first one, then the other, as if he were watching a tennis match. "Sounds good to me," he said, grateful he had these two crazy women in his life.

"I will have a stake in the profits, of course," Anna said.

"Of course," he said.

"I have a feeling the second store is just the beginning for Brian's Books & Coffee Shop," Anna said, beaming. "And I intend to turn a pretty penny on this deal when I sell it back to you in a few years."

"And the house is yours to do what you want with, isn't it?" Luanne said.

"Yep."

"After all," Luanne said. "She did hate the place."

"Yes, she did," Brian said. "But, in the end, Michelle was fair. Now, ladies, if you'll excuse me. I have to get back to Annapolis."

"Wait!" Luanne protested. "Stay and eat lunch, Brian. I have a funny story to tell you."

"A funny story?" Brian said. "Can't it wait until later?"

"It's about Chip Matthews."

Brian sat down and gazed at his mother. "I'm all ears," he said.

The waiter arrived and they ordered crab cake sandwiches for everyone while Brian waited impatiently. "So?" he said after they were alone again. "What about Skip?"

"You mean Chip?" Luanne corrected, and Brian shrugged.

"Well," Anna said. "I just happened to be in this restaurant in Baltimore. I saw Chip there with a lovely young woman—skinny little thing, eating a salad. Well, of course, I stopped by their table to say hello. Chip looked at me as if I were Bux McGee coming to arrest him. Well, you know me, I just had to introduce myself because Chip gave no signs of introducing me to his lunch companion. Her name was Melanie Mary Murphy—lyrical, isn't it? Of course, I asked Melanie Mary Murphy the burning question: 'Are you a friend of Chip's, my dear?' She looked at me as if I had two heads and explained that she and Chip are engaged to be married. I told her that Melanie Mary Murphy Matthews was a lovely name. I may even ask her if I can use it in my next book.

"Anyhoo, she asked me where I knew Chip from and I told her about the article that was written about Brian's store. We talked about it at length, particularly the part where he asked Jenny for a date. According to

Melanie Mary Murphy, Chip's editor is forever making him plant little flirtations into his articles. The editor thinks it keeps the lady readers entertained.

"Of course, I couldn't bear to spill the beans. I'd grown rather fond of Melanie quite quickly, and I wouldn't dream of hurting her feelings. But it was comical watching the look of horror on Chip's face. He kept saying things like, 'I know you must be very busy, Miss Waters. We don't want to keep you, Miss Waters.' I laughed all the way to the car."

"Car?" Brian asked. "You don't drive, Anna."

"Oh, I drove her," Luanne said.

"To a restaurant in Baltimore? When?"

Luanne and Anna glanced nervously at each other for a second. "Er . . . we just happened to be at the offices of the newspaper. We were questioning . . . er . . . talking with some of Chip's coworkers. It was a pure coincidence."

"I'm sure it was," Brian said. "Does Jenny know about this?"

"Yes," Anna said. "I told her. She took it well. She said she'd always suspected there was something underhanded about Chip—I think we've all harbored similar suspicions. Chip coincidentally called Jenny. Naturally, she told him that she wished him nothing but the best in his future endeavors. She also told him that if he ever called her again, she'd make a phone call of her own to Melanie Mary Murphy and set her straight about a thing or two."

"That's awful," Brian said.

"Not at all," Anna said. "Jenny never really cared for

Chip, deep down. She was flattered by his attention and she was hoping she could help me sell more books. But Chip wasn't her type. Finding out he was engaged was just what she needed to hear."

The crab cake sandwiches arrived just then, and Brian picked his up off his plate and wrapped it in a napkin.

"I'll take this with me," he said, giving both women a quick peck on the cheek.

"Where are you going?" Luanne protested.

"I've got to get back to Annapolis," he said. "It's Friday."

"What's the rush?" Anna said.

"I've got something I need to take care of," he said, before he bolted for the door.

Anna and Luanne watched him through the big plate glass window as he passed by. They both wore big smiles.

Chapter Twenty-eight

Brian knew that he should be thankful his troubles were over, but the sense of liberation that he longed for was missing. Of course, he was sad about the divorce—not sad that the marriage was over, but sad that he'd failed to make his marriage work. He thought back to the way he felt watching Michelle walk out the door of their home that night. It seemed like the end of the world at the time. Little did he know, it was the best thing that could have happened to both of them.

He looked at his watch. Where was Jenny?

Brian picked up the telephone for the tenth time since he'd gotten back to the store, but he put it down again. He'd dialed her number a few times, but ended up hanging up every time. Was she hurt by Chip? Did she need some space to think things through? Would his call only make her more confused? Brian knew first-hand that time was a great healer of wounded feelings.

He'd practiced what he wanted to say, but it never sounded quite right. "I'm not Chip," he would tell her. "I'd never lie to you. I'd never hurt you."

Brian watched the clock tick away the minutes. Fifteen minutes to go until closing time. Ten. Five. It was time to lock up the store but, somehow, he couldn't do it.

The bells on the front door chimed and he looked up anxiously just in time to see her finally coming through the door.

"Hi," he said.

"Hi."

"How's it going?"

"Good," she said.

"I've been waiting for you."

"I thought you might be," she said. "I got here as soon as I could. I'm painting a mural for the new seafood restaurant downtown and I'm behind schedule. It won't take long for me to pick out a book. I'll just grab a mystery and get out of your way."

"You're not in my way," Brian said, and instead of letting her go to the book racks, he followed her. "Jenny, wait!"

She stopped and turned around, looking at him with earnest blue eyes.

"Wait," he said again. "I wanted to tell you that I'm sorry."

"What are you sorry for, Brian?"

"I'm sorry I didn't call you this week. I'm sorry that Chip-Skip was a jerk."

"Oh, that," she said and rolled her eyes. "I always

thought there was something a little snarky about that guy. Don't be sorry about Chip, Brian. It wasn't as if we had a romance."

"He wanted a romance with you."

"That's what he said, anyway. It turns out he was already in one—a small detail he forgot to mention. Not that I have a right to criticize. I'd already told Chip I was happy to show him around Annapolis, but that . . . I told him I was waiting for someone."

Brian said nothing. He didn't have to, because he already knew. Jenny had been waiting for him. "Why?" he asked, moving closer to her.

"Why, what?" she asked.

"Why would you wait for . . . me?" He didn't let her answer. Instead he took her in his arms and held her. "Why would a woman like you wait for someone like me to resolve a mountain of stupid mistakes? Why me, Jenny?"

"Because," she said, falling into his arms. "Because you never lied to me about your life and because you're worth the wait." They looked into each other's eyes, arms wrapped around each other. Suddenly, there was the clatter of the bells on the door.

"We're closed," he called, not taking his eyes off Jenny.

"Sorry," a voice said. "I'll come back tomorrow." Then he heard the bells jingle again.

"I'd better go," Jenny said, pulling away.

"But you didn't pick a book."

"Oh, yeah," she said and then smiled. "I sort of fibbed about needing a mystery book. I still haven't read the one I bought last week. I'll see you tomorrow. Anna is having everyone over for crabs."

"Again?" Brian said. "No wonder there's a shortage."

She grinned and kissed him on the cheek. "I'll see you there."

"Wait . . ." he called as she began to walk away. "Did you hear the news?"

"What news?"

"Anna didn't tell you?"

"No," Jenny said.

"I thought for sure either she or my mother would have called you by now."

"Nope. No one called. What's the news?"

"My divorce is final."

Her eyes lit up for a fleeting second. "Really?" she said.

"Yep. Michelle signed the papers today."

"No. I didn't hear. Should I say congratulations or I'm sorry?"

"I don't know," he confessed.

"I'm sorry."

"No. I think congratulations fits better."

"I'm still sorry you went through the pain."

"Thank you, but it's over and I'm relieved. Would you mind waiting while I lock up? I'd love a pepperoni pizza. I won't take no for an answer."

"Good," Jenny said. "I don't want you to."

They looked at each other for another long moment, and then they both started to laugh. "You must think I'm nuts!" Brian said at last.

"Maybe a little," she confessed, and gave him another beautiful smile.

"What do you say? Mario's is open." He studied her expression intently, knowing he'd never wanted a pepperoni pizza more in his life.

"Why not?" she said with a shrug.

She waited for him as he locked up, talking good-naturedly about the new bookstore that would soon be opening. He turned off the lights and led her to the front door. Then he stopped and looked at her.

"Did you forget something?" she asked.

"Yes."

"What is it?"

"This," he said, and kissed her. She melted into his arms and he held her tightly, kissing her mouth and her eyes and her neck. Holding her and kissing her the way he'd been wanting to for a long, long time.

"We'd better go," she said finally, pulling away. "I'm starved."

"Me too," Brian said, and opened the door. They stepped into the cool, clear night and he locked the door.

For a moment Brian let his mind wander and he thought about all of the wonderful things he and Jenny would do. He took her hand in his and held it as they walked. He liked the way it felt inside of his as he led her down the street. He never wanted to let it go.

"So you don't like romance novels?" he chided gently as they walked. She said nothing, but the twinkle in her eyes told him that she might be open to a new type of mystery.

Someday, Brian thought to himself as they turned the corner toward the restaurant, he would confess to Jenny that he sometimes read romance novels and that, yes, she was right, he was a dreamer after all.